The mere idea of being close to this man shook her senses.

Behind that incredibly masculine face and rock-hard body, he was a lawman. How could Noelle be attracted to him?

She couldn't answer that. She only knew that for the first time in years, Evan was making her remember that she was a woman. And the feeling was too good to pass up.

"I thought you might enjoy seeing something other than that little ranch of yours," he said with a lazy grin.

Since she'd moved she'd been asked out on a few dates. She'd refused all of them. And something told her if she was smart now, she'd tell Evan Calhoun a loud, decisive no.

But something strange was going on inside her. For the life of her she couldn't seem to form the word, much less say it to the man.

* * *

Men of the West:
Whether ranchers or lawmen, these heartbreakers can ride, shoot—and drive a woman crazy...

Dear Reader,

Christmas is coming to the Silver Horn Ranch, and this year one of the Calhoun brothers has more on his mind than buying gifts for his family. Ever since Evan woke up in a dry gulch with lovely Noelle's face hovered over his, the rugged lawman has had one thing on his mind—how to make the ranching woman a permanent fixture in his life.

I've always loved Christmas. Being with my family, cooking, tree trimming, the crowded stores and even waiting in long checkout lines make the season special for me. But when it comes to gift buying, I always start agonizing whether I've spent too little, too much, or picked out something that's totally inappropriate. As for Evan, he believes he's found the perfect gift to give his lady, but he soon gets a lesson in Christmas giving and what the meaning of love is all about.

I hope you'll join me in celebrating Christmas in Nevada, and I hope that each and every one of you has a blessed holiday filled with love and happiness.

Merry Christmas!

Stella Bagwell

The Lawman's Noelle

Stella Bagwell

Recycling programs
for this product may
not exist in your area.

ISBN-13: 978-0-373-65857-2

The Lawman's Noelle

Copyright © 2014 by Stella Bagwell

Printed in U.S.A.

www.Harlequin.com

STELLA BAGWELL

has written more than seventy novels for Harlequin. She credits her loyal readers and hopes her stories have brightened their lives in some small way. A cowgirl through and through, she loves to watch old Westerns and has recently learned how to rope a steer. Her days begin and end helping her husband care for a beloved herd of horses on their little ranch located on the south Texas coast. When she's not ropin' and ridin', you'll find her at her desk, creating her next tale of love. The couple has a son, who is a high school math teacher and athletic coach. Stella loves to hear from readers and invites them to contact her at stellabagwell@gmail.com.

To all my friends at Jim's Big Burgers.
Thank you for the brownies, coffee and food.
And most of all, for making us feel special.

Chapter One

Reining the bay horse to a stop on the rocky rise, Noelle Barnes stood in her stirrups and peered toward the dry wash more than a hundred yards below. The dark lump lying near those slabs of rock looked like a man! And he wasn't moving!

Was he injured or sick? Or even dead?

Her adrenaline pumping, Noelle quickly guided her horse, Driller, down the rocky slope. Along the way, she buried the lower half of her face in the woolen muffler tied around her neck and tried to ignore the early December wind whipping across the bare Nevada hills. The frigid air permeated her heavy brown ranch coat and caused her eyes to water, but she was used to being out in brutal weather. And she could hardly turn back now!

Halfway to the gulch, a sinking feeling hit the pit of her stomach. Her eyes hadn't deceived her. The object lying at the bottom of the wash wasn't an animal. It was a person!

Urging her horse to a faster gait, she wound her way downward through the rocks and sage until she reached the bank of the deep gulch. By then she could see a man lying facedown in the gravel.

Oh, my! Was he dead? What was he doing way out here? Alone?

Her heart pounding with fear, she guided Driller over the ledge and down the steep embankment. The ground was loose and the horse's hind feet slid in several places, but at that moment she wasn't concerned about either of them falling. Driller was sure-footed, and she'd ridden a horse for nearly all of her twenty-eight years.

"Come on, boy," she encouraged her trusted mount. "A little farther and we'll have it made."

Noelle had hardly gotten the words out of her mouth when, several yards up the draw, another horse nickered shrilly. Driller returned the greeting.

"We'll find your friend later," she told Driller. "Right now we need to see if we have a corpse on our hands."

At the bottom of the wash, Noelle dismounted. After tying Driller's reins to a dead juniper trunk, she hurried over to the motionless body.

Dropping to her knees, she leaned over him, but stopped short of touching any part of him. Only a portion of the left side of his face was visible, yet it was enough for Noelle to discern he was young—somewhere in his thirties—and clean-shaven. A trickle of blood oozed through the dark chestnut hair just above his ear.

Jerking off her leather glove, she shoved away the kerchief tied around his neck and felt for a pulse. Relief flooded through her as she detected a faint but steady beat.

"Hey, mister, can you hear me? Wake up and tell me what happened."

With her property being so remote, it wasn't much use carrying a cell phone. She would either try to move this man on her own or go for help. And considering that he appeared to be at least six feet tall and somewhere close to a hundred and eighty pounds, she figured throwing him over his horse would be a mighty big chore.

Racing back to Driller, she jerked a bottle of water and a piece of ragged towel from her saddlebags. "He's out, Driller. Colder than a mackerel. If I can't wake him up, you and I might have to ride like hell to get help."

Noelle raced back to the downed man, while behind her, the horse pawed as though to tell her he understood. And she'd bet that he did. Living out here for nearly four years, with no one to talk to but her animals, she figured they'd all learned a vast human vocabulary.

The water was slushy with ice. She poured a bit onto the rag and placed it on the man's forehead, then shook his shoulder.

"Mister, can you hear me?" she practically yelled. "You need to wake up so I can get you out of this gulch."

The shock of the water coupled with her voice must have done the trick, because he suddenly moaned and attempted to lift his head from the gravel bed.

Tossing the cold cloth aside, she slipped a hand beneath his head and lowered it to the ground. "Whoa, there. Just lie still for a minute."

He continued to stir. As his head moved slowly back and forth, his eyelids fluttered open. Noelle had never been so glad to see a pair of dark green eyes, even if they weren't totally focused.

"Oh, hell—I hurt all over." Lifting a hand to the wound on the side of his head, he gazed groggily up at her. "Who are you?"

"Noelle Barnes. My property runs along the east side of this gulch. I spotted you from up on the ridge. Do you know what happened?"

Appearing to gather more steam, he braced a hand against the ground and, with Noelle supporting his shoulder, he pushed himself to a sitting position. "My head feels like someone used a claw hammer on it."

"No doubt. You have a goose egg and a gash just above your ear. I'm not a doctor, but I'm guessing you have a concussion, at least. You can move your arms and legs, so that's a good sign. Still, you need to get to a hospital."

He swiped a hand across his face and Noelle used the moment to gather more details about the man. He was dressed in dark blue jeans and a pair of brown ostrich-leather boots that probably cost more than she would spend on food for the next six months. His heavy, olive green jacket was made of oiled canvas, and beneath the corduroy collar was a white shirt. Although he looked natural in the cowboy gear, he appeared far too neat to be a working rancher.

"I'll worry about that later." He turned his head stiffly in an effort to look behind him. "Right now, do you see my hat anywhere? And what about my horse?"

"You sit still," she ordered him. "I'll round up both of them."

She found the tan felt hat a few feet from where he'd fallen. The left side of the crown was bent in and the brim smeared with dirt, but that was the least of this man's problems at the moment. She wasn't at all sure he was feeling up to riding anywhere.

Thankfully, the horse, a black-and-white paint, wasn't far away. The moment he spotted Noelle, he walked right up to her, as though he'd already decided he and his saddle pal needed help.

After gathering his reins, she gave the animal several reassuring pats on the neck, then led him through a tangle of sagebrush and rock until they reached the man. He was still sitting on the ground, his head hanging between his knees.

"Here's your hat and your horse," she told him. "But I'd advise you to stay where you are and get your bearings before you try to stand up."

He turned an accusing eye on the horse. "This is the first time a horse has dumped me in years. That's what I get for trusting my brother when I asked him for a mount."

Noelle didn't attempt to figure out that last remark. Instead, she got straight to the point. "Do you remember what happened?"

"I do now. A sage hen or some kind of bird flew up right in front of our faces, and it must have scared the devil out of the horse. Before I knew what was happening, he was walking on his hind legs, and I was headed toward the ground. I must have hit my head on a rock or something. That's all I know until I woke up and found you standing over me."

The man was an attractive son of a gun, she thought, but not in the pretty-boy kind of way her old girlfriends down in Phoenix used to swoon over. No, this man's features were too harsh and rugged to be described as handsome or anything close to it. But the dark rusty hair falling onto his forehead was as sexy as all get-out, and so were his green eyes.

"What are you doing out here, anyway?" she asked. "This is private land."

He reached inside his coat and pulled out a leather wallet. When he flipped it open and flashed a lawman's badge at her, everything inside Noelle went cold and stiff.

If the man hadn't been injured, she would've climbed on Driller and rode away without a backward glance.

But he was dazed and hurt, and she wouldn't turn her back on anyone who needed help. Even a lawman.

"Detective Evan Calhoun, Carson City Sheriff's Office," she read aloud. "What's a detective doing out here on my land?"

"Your land? I was on government lease, following four-wheeler tracks. I crossed over a downed fence because the tracks continued into this gulch. I never thought the fence was a boundary line. Most landowners try to keep those upright."

She huffed out a heavy breath. "The fence on the other side of this draw does need work," she admitted. "I've been using the gulch as a boundary fence."

"Well, sorry about getting onto your land." He pushed up the cuff of his jacket and squinted at a gold watch. "Damn. I've been out here way too long."

He made a move to get to his feet. Noelle felt compelled to grab his arm and give him a steady pull. Once he was standing, he swayed slightly, but with her supporting him, he managed to stay upright.

"Between the freezing weather and that whack on the head, it's a wonder you haven't gone into shock," she told him.

His gaze focused directly on her face, and Noelle felt something in her stomach do a crazy flip.

"I'm grateful that you found me," he said. "What did you say your name was?"

"Barnes. Noelle Barnes."

"Miss? Mrs.?"

She tried not to bristle at the question. It wasn't really any of his business whether she was married or single. But maybe he was thinking she had a husband back at the house who could help. Only Noelle didn't have a husband. She didn't even have a cell phone.

"Ms.," she answered curtly.

He extended his hand to her. "Well, thank you very much, Ms. Barnes. If not for you, I might still be on the cold ground."

Even with the leather acting as a barrier between their skin, the feel of his strong hand wrapping around hers was very unsettling. Her reaction had nothing to do with him being a detective for the sheriff's office.

She looked away to a spot at the far end of the gulch. "No need for thanks. Do you think you're up for a short ride? My house is only a couple of miles from here. Where did you leave your truck and trailer?"

"Farther than that. It's parked just off a county road a few miles north of here."

She eased her hand from his. "Then you'd better come with me and rest before you head on home."

"My vision is still a little blurred, but my head is clearing. I think I can ride back to my truck all right." He pulled a cell phone from a leather holder on his belt and squinted at the flat screen, then muttered something under his breath. "I'm having trouble focusing, but it looks to me like I'm not receiving a signal of any kind. This thing is useless out here."

"Which is why I never bother with one," she replied.

He jammed the phone back into the holder. "Okay, I'll forget that plan. If you'd be kind enough to call the sheriff's office when you get home, just let them know I'm okay and will be getting back late."

In spite of being uncomfortable in this man's presence, she shook her head. He hardly looked well enough to ride to his truck. It was going to be difficult for him even to get to her house.

"Forget it," she said flatly. "I'd be stupider than you are if I let you ride off in the condition you're in."

"Look, Ms. Barnes, I—"

"Call me Noelle. And right now you're in no shape to argue. If necessary, I figure I could manhandle you." She pulled his horse forward and slipped the reins over the animal's neck. "See if you can mount up. We're going to my place."

Apparently deciding he might be smart to take her advice, he took a step toward the horse and immediately swayed. Noelle grabbed his arm to prevent him from collapsing. With his chin resting on his chest, he pulled in several long breaths.

"I think you might be right," he said in a strained voice. "I don't feel so great."

Fearing he was going to pass out, she slipped an arm around his waist and held him tightly. "Do you need to sit down? There's no hurry. We can try this in a few minutes."

"No. Just let me get my foot in the stirrup and then give me a shove up."

If nothing else, he was determined, Noelle thought. She twisted the stirrup around to give him easier access. "I hope your paint doesn't decide to move. He might end up dragging you into the next county."

"If he does, I'll come back to haunt my brother Finn," he muttered.

To her relief, he managed to get his foot in the stirrup. With one hand against his back and the other on his butt, she pushed until he plopped into the saddle with a heavy thud.

Hurrying around to the right side of the horse, she fixed his other boot into the stirrup, then handed him the reins. By now he was half slumped over the saddle horn, his face the color of putty.

"Are you going to fall off?" she asked with concern.

He responded with a dismissive wave. "Get your horse. I'll make it."

There was nothing more she could do now, Noelle decided as she hurried over to Driller. Except pray that he could hang on long enough to reach the warmth and safety of her house.

Once in the saddle, she turned Driller down the draw. The paint obediently fell into step behind her. Thank God the horse wasn't behaving like a wild bronco. Now she had to find an easier trail for them to climb the steep bank of the gulch. Otherwise, the lawman might tumble off his horse again. She seriously doubted his head could survive another impact.

Unfortunately, as the draw narrowed, the steepness of the bank increased. A hundred yards from where they'd started, she pulled Driller to a stop to look back at the lawman. If the situation hadn't been so serious, she would've been inclined to smile at the cockeyed angle of his hat and the dazed look on his face. But a head injury could be deadly. She wanted to get him out of the cold and to medical help as quickly as she could.

"Looks like we'd better climb the cut bank here before the trail gets any steeper," she told him. "And hang on. I don't want to have to pick you up off the ground and throw you over the saddle."

"Yes, ma'am. Just lead on."

The climb made three switchbacks through a patch of scrubby juniper and creosote bushes. Throughout the ascent, Noelle kept glancing behind her, expecting at any moment to see him listing precariously from one side of the horse to the other. But thankfully, he managed to keep his seat until they reached the top. She sighed with relief.

From this point on, the trail wasn't nearly as challenging. Barring an incident with his horse, they'd be at her place in a half hour. And then what was she going to do with him?

As the horses clopped along at a steady walk, Evan focused on Noelle Barnes's back. Although his vision wasn't completely clear yet, he could see she was bundled in heavy clothing. A worn, brown ranch coat topped her faded jeans, while a red woolen muffler was looped several times around her neck. The old gray felt hat on her head sported a ring of sweat stains around the band. The flattened brim was covered with dust. Long, dark hair fell about her shoulders, and each step of the horse caused it to swish against her back.

What was she doing out here on this cold December day? he wondered. She'd said this was her property. Even so, it was hardly the type of weather in which to take a leisurely ride. She wore long shank spurs on her boots, something a novice rider would never do, and she handled her mount as though being atop a horse was as familiar as walking across the kitchen floor.

One thing was for sure. She wasn't the soft, delicate sort or anything close to the type of woman he occasionally dated. While he'd been sitting on the ground trying to get his bearings, he'd noticed she was rather tall, with some weight on her bones. Her figure was shapely enough to fill a man's head with all sorts of pleasurable thoughts. But it had been her face that caught his complete attention.

The cold wind had whipped a rosy color into her cheeks and turned her wide lips a pale pink. Large chocolate-brown eyes had studied him with unashamed candor, and it had become apparent to Evan that she was a woman who followed her own rules.

As the two horses carried them through a series of low hills covered with sparse tufts of grass and patches of sagebrush, thoughts of Noelle Barnes continued to slip in and out of his groggy mind. Normally Evan would've used this opportunity to toss a pile of questions at her. But with pain still beating at the backs of his eyes, it was all he could do to stay upright in the saddle.

Fifteen minutes into the ride, they passed a herd of cattle numbering a hundred or more. Evan wondered whether they belonged to Noelle Barnes, but he lacked the strength to ask her. A quarter of a mile later, a small house came into view. The run-down stucco sat on a knoll and was a faded beige that matched the color of the dead vegetation covering the land around it.

Several yards behind the house stood a big barn of weathered gray wood. The loft was open at the end, and he could see it was practically full of alfalfa hay. Next to the structure were several corrals, some of them made of wooden rails, the others crudely built with cedar posts bound closely. A cow with a small calf was in one of the pens, while two horses were stalled next to them.

Yep, there was definitely a man around, Evan thought with a measure of relief. This woman wouldn't be ranching out here alone. It just wasn't possible.

He followed her to an old hitching post erected a few feet in front of the barn. Nearby, the penned horses lifted their heads and nickered at their buddy. Other than that, nothing stirred.

Evan glanced from the barn area over toward the house. "Where's your help?"

"You're looking at it," she said bluntly. "Get down and I'll take you to the house before I deal with the horses."

Evan wasn't used to having a woman order him around. Normally he would've been irked by Noelle Barnes's bossy attitude. But he was too busy thinking about her being out here alone to dwell on her brusque commands.

He climbed to the ground. As soon as his boots were firmly on the hard dirt, he was stunned to feel his knees shaking with weakness. Evan had always been a fairly healthy guy with hardly a sick day in his life. Feeling this vulnerable was something he'd never experienced. It jarred him to the very core of his being.

"I'm feeling better," he said in the strongest voice he could muster. "And I need to leave my horse saddled. I've got a long ride from here."

"You're not riding anywhere."

Not wanting to argue the matter and waste what little strength he had, he simply handed her the reins.

After she'd tethered both horses at the hitching rail, he followed her across the barren yard to a back porch with a low roof supported by cedar posts. The door opened directly into a small kitchen. As Evan stepped in behind her, he caught the scent of burned coffee and cooked apples.

Rough-hewn beams supported the room's low ceiling, while the floor was covered with worn brown linoleum. A green curtain with roosters printed across the hem hung over the only window. Below it, a chipped porcelain sink was full of dirty dishes.

"Sit at the table and let me take another look at your head," she said. "Looks like it's still bleeding."

Evan walked over to a white farm table pushed against the back wall of the room and removed his coat before he sank into a chair at the end.

"I'll be right back," she said.

He watched her leave the room, then glanced curiously around him. Where was the phone? Surely she had a landline somewhere. He had to call in to the office. His coworkers had probably been trying to contact him for the past two hours.

The thought had him pulling his phone from its holder, but as soon as he turned it on, he mentally cursed. The signal was no stronger here than it had been in the dry gulch.

Deciding he didn't have time to wait for the woman with the velvety brown eyes, he pushed himself to his feet and moved, albeit shakily, toward the open doorway she'd disappeared through.

He'd taken two steps into a tiny hallway when she suddenly stepped from a door on his right and nearly rammed right into him.

"What the hell are you doing?" she barked at him. "I told you to sit!"

He understood this whole ordeal was a nuisance and a huge interruption to her day, but he didn't deserve this. Nor had he asked for it.

Squinting, he focused his aching eyes on her face. "I admit I got a wham on the head, but as far as I can tell, I still have my memory. I don't recall you being my boss."

Her lips, which had turned a darker pink since they'd entered the warm house, pressed into a thin line of disgust.

"I'm not trying to be your boss. I'm trying to keep you from falling on your face and reinjuring yourself." She made a sweeping motion toward the front part of the house. "But be my guest and roam around all you want. If you need me, I'll be in the kitchen."

With that, she started to walk away, but he snatched a hold on her forearm. She met his reaction with a questioning stare that had him immediately dropping his hand to his side.

"Sorry. Just tell me where the phone is. I'll make a call and get myself out of your hair."

She pointed to the right, where a doorway opened to another room. "In there. At the end of the couch."

"Thank you. I—" Before he could finish, a wave of woozy weakness came over him. He instinctively reached out to her to brace himself.

He heard her mutter a curse under her breath as she grabbed his arm to steady him. "Come on," she said in a gentler tone. "I'll help you to the phone."

With a supporting hand on his arm, she guided him out of the hallway and into a cozy living room. Along the way, he noticed she'd taken off the ranch coat, and he was surprised to catch the faint, mellowed scent of flowers emanating from the wool sweater she wore. The garment was tattered at the neck and the cuffs, and the Nordic weave across her breasts had faded. She hadn't bothered with makeup or fussed with her clothing, but she'd taken time that morning to put on a feminine scent. Evan had always found it difficult to understand a woman's thinking, but this lady was far too complex for him even to try to unravel.

He sank heavily onto the cushion of a short red couch. Noelle handed him a cordless phone from a nearby table.

"I'll look at your head after you finish your call. Do you think you can drink something? Water? Coffee or hot chocolate?"

She was standing in front of him, her legs slightly apart and one hand resting on her hip. The faded denim outlined her strong thighs and rounded hips, while the sweater clung to her breasts. She was more woman than he'd ever had in his arms. In spite of the throbbing pain in his head, he had to admit to himself that there was something very sexy and sensual about her.

"Do you have any aspirin? I'd take two of those with a cup of coffee."

"You think it's wise to medicate yourself?"

He reached up and tentatively touched his fingertips to the lump above his ear. "I'll make sure the doctor knows—whenever I see him."

"You're going to see him as soon as I can drive you into town. So make your call. I'll be back in a few minutes." She turned to leave the room.

He quickly asked, "You're planning on taking me to town?"

She frowned at him. "That's right. You're not up to riding or driving. How else would you get there?"

He did his best to straighten his shoulders. "There's no need for you to trouble yourself. I'm about to call my office. Someone will drive out to pick me up."

"No," she blurted. "I don't want any more lawmen around here."

Although each word he spoke seemed to intensify the ache in his head, he attempted to joke, "What's the matter? Is there a stack of warrants out on you or something?"

Her nostrils flared as she stared at him. "No. I simply don't like you people. That's all."

Too stunned to make any sort of reply, Evan watched her walk out of the room.

You people? Through the ten years he'd worked for the sheriff's office, he'd met plenty of folks who disliked lawmen. But they were usually drunks, drug users or hardened criminals. Not a decent woman like Noelle Barnes.

What had a lawman ever done to her? he wondered. Put her in jail? Broken her heart?

Mentally shaking his aching head, Evan punched in his partner's cell number and lifted the phone to his ear.

It didn't matter whether Noelle Barnes loved or hated law officials, he told himself. Once he got back to civilization, he'd never see her again.

Chapter Two

More than an hour later, as Noelle paced restlessly around the large waiting area of the hospital emergency unit, she was still trying to figure out what had come over her.

Like Evan had told her, there'd been no real reason for her to drive him into town or to see that he got to a doctor. There were plenty of deputies in the sheriff's office who would've come to Noelle's house and collected him. Instead, she'd insisted she drive him herself. Now, as the long minutes continued to tick by, she began to worry that his injury might have been more serious than either of them had suspected.

She'd seen people before who had taken severe licks on the head. Once her brother, Andy, had been hit in the temple with a hard-thrown baseball, but the only bad effect he'd suffered was a black eye. Then a girlfriend of hers had fallen and banged her head against a concrete wall while she and Noelle were roller-skating. But the only injury she'd sustained was a minor cut on the scalp.

On the drive into town, Evan Calhoun had told her that his mother had died from a head injury after a simple fall on the staircase. And though he didn't appear to be connecting her demise with his own injury, just hearing about it had shaken Noelle. No matter whether he worked as a carpenter, a cowboy or a law officer, she didn't want anything bad to happen to him.

The sound of a crying baby drew Noelle's attention. Across the room, a young woman was trying to pacify a fussy infant and control a rowdy toddler at the same time. The mother looked completely frazzled, yet Noelle couldn't help but envy the woman. She had someone to love, someone who needed her. She had a family.

Jamming her hands into the front pockets of her jeans, Noelle looked down at her boots and tried to keep her mind from slipping back to Phillip and the short year they'd been married. For a while, she'd been naively in love. Like most new brides, she'd been dreaming and planning for their future. One with two or three children they would raise on a small ranch outside Phoenix. But those wonderful dreams had been flattened when she'd discovered Phillip was as phony as her father's integrity.

With a weary sigh, she looked away from the mother and children and glanced for the umpteenth time at the double doors where Evan had disappeared with a nurse. He'd been back there nearly two hours. Something had to be dreadfully wrong.

Determined it was high time to get some answers, she marched over to the admission desk, where two nurses were dealing with ringing phones, paperwork and people who were just as weary and worried as she.

Trying to hold on to the slender thread of patience she had left, Noelle was waiting in line to speak with one of the nurses when the double doors suddenly opened. Relief flooded through her as she spotted Evan in a wheelchair, being pushed by a male nurse. Evan looked pale and wrung out, but that was far better than lying flat on his back in a hospital bed.

Stepping out of the slow-moving line of people, she intercepted the two men before they reached the middle of the waiting area.

"The doctor isn't holding you over?" she asked in surprise. For the past half hour, she'd been thinking he'd be admitted to a room for a night of observation, at the very least.

"No, thank God." He slanted her a weak grin. "I didn't think you'd still be here."

She lifted her chin. "Why would I run out on you? I've already wasted most of the day. What's two more hours?"

He chuckled before cringing in pain. Noelle was surprised at how much empathy she felt for him. Up until she'd found him in the gulch with his face in the gravel bed, she'd never met him. Having this much concern for a complete stranger wasn't normal.

Out of the corner of her eye, she could see the nurse making a survey of her rough work clothes and dusty hat. No doubt he wondered what connection she had to this Carson City detective.

"Are you taking this man home?" the nurse asked Noelle.

"That's right."

"Then park your vehicle next to the curb and I'll bring him out."

Noelle exited the building and hurried to fetch her truck. Cold wind swept across the crowded parking lot. She tried not to imagine what would've happened if she'd ridden in a different direction today. Even if Evan had awakened without her help, he might not have been physically capable of tracking down his horse and riding out of the gulch on his own. The plummeting temperature tonight would've surely caused him to suffer hypothermia. Noelle had always believed that things happened for a reason. It was clear that she was meant to rescue the detective, although she couldn't imagine why.

A few minutes later, after Evan was safely buckled in the passenger seat and she had the heater blowing on their feet, she put the vehicle in motion.

"Okay, you need to give me a clue where you live," she told him as she directed the truck toward the nearest exit of the parking lot. "I'm not familiar with the residential streets around Carson City, so you might start with some general directions."

"Sorry, but I don't live here in town. Just take me by the sheriff's office. Someone there can drive me home."

Glancing over, she saw that he'd removed his hat. The hair around the wound had been clipped down to the scalp, and a row of stitches now held the gashed skin together. The man was tough to be up and walking, she thought. She'd give him that much.

"Is there some reason you're trying to get rid of me?" she asked.

Wiping a hand over his face, he said, "No. Just trying to save you a long trip. I'm sure you have things to do at home."

"The daylight hours are gone. The only thing I'm going to do when I get home is feed the horses and tend to a sick cow."

He didn't say anything until the traffic cleared enough for her to pull into the street. "Okay. Go to 395 and head north."

Noelle didn't know why she'd made it her responsibility to see this man to the doctor and then home. She could have let a coworker deal with him. But something about finding him on her property and rescuing him from hypothermia, or worse, had left her feeling a bit possessive. Like finding a wounded animal and not wanting to let go until she was certain it could survive without help.

"A deputy has already gone out and collected my truck and trailer from where I parked them on the side of the road," he informed her. "Someone will pick up my horse tomorrow. And don't worry, it won't be a lawman. It'll be someone from the ranch."

She darted another glance at him. This time his eyes were shut, his head resting against the back of the seat. Even with that angry wound above his ear and a pale face, he still managed to look incredibly strong and handsome.

Unable to contain her curiosity, she asked, "You have a ranch?"

"It belongs to my family."

"So you do ranch work along with being a detective for the sheriff's office?"

"Since about ten years ago, I haven't done much cowboy work. That's when I started working as a deputy."

He was telling her that he lived on the ranch but didn't work there. How did that situation sit with the rest of his family? she wondered. And what kind of family did this man have? Did it include a wife and children? Somehow she didn't think so. He didn't have the look of a man who'd been roped and tied by a woman.

What the heck has come over you, Noelle? Whether this man, or any man, is married should mean nothing to you. You don't want one in your life. He wouldn't be worth the heartache.

Shutting her mind to the mocking voice in her head, she asked, "What did the doctor say about your injury? They kept you back there so long I thought you must've been going through brain surgery."

"Sorry you had such a long wait. After the doc finally studied the scans of my head, he said I have a concussion. He prescribed something for the pain and ordered me to take it easy the next few days. And not to get another lick on the head. I told him I wouldn't be riding Lonesome anytime soon."

Lonesome. The horse's name fit Noelle perfectly, she thought. Aloud she said, "I liked your paint. You wouldn't think about selling him to me, would you?"

Out of the corner of her eye, she could see him looking at her with comical surprise. "Are you kidding me?"

"I don't do much kidding, Detective Calhoun."

"My name is Evan. Call me that, will you?"

In her mind, she'd already been calling him Evan. But he hardly needed to know she'd been thinking about him in such a familiar way. "All right, Evan. Now what about the horse? While I was unsaddling him, I looked him over. He has big strong bones, great withers and a nice soft eye. The two of us have already decided we like each other."

He studied her for a long, thoughtful moment before he finally replied, "I'll have to ask my brother. He handles the ranch's remuda."

She frowned as she maneuvered the truck into the passing lane. "Your ranch has a remuda?"

"Why, yes. Every ranch has a remuda."

She supposed he was technically right. Even a small spread like hers needed a horse. Only the word *remuda* meant a collective string of them. And her string consisted of three.

"Now that we're talking about ranching," he went on, "I'm still trying to figure out if I heard you right today. You work that place of yours all by yourself?"

"That's right. I can't afford help. And even if I could, I prefer doing things my own way and at my own pace."

He lifted his head to look at her. Though she could see him only in her peripheral vision, the sight was enough to rattle her senses. Without even trying, he was one of the sexiest men she'd ever crossed paths with. Being confined in the truck cab with him reminded her just how long it had been since she'd felt a man's arms around her.

"How do you manage it all alone?" he asked. "As we rode to your house, I spotted a fairly large herd of cattle."

He sounded clearly astounded. Noelle figured the women in his life were probably a different breed from her. Most likely they were the soft, delicate sort who looked great in lingerie but acted helpless in a feed-lot. Sometimes in the quiet darkness of the night, she wished she could be that woman, if only for an hour or two. But that wouldn't pay the bills or put food on the table. She had to be strong and capable. Always.

"Only a hundred fifty head. Doesn't take much work to feed that many cattle in the winter. In the summer, when grass is available, I can concentrate on other things. And when it comes time for branding and working, I call on the day hands who work over on the Double X."

"Hmm. So how long have you had your place?"

Ever since her beloved aunt and uncle had died and her snake-in-the-grass ex had shown his true colors, she thought grimly. To Evan, she said, "Four years— give or take a few months. My aunt Geneva and uncle Rob willed it to me with the stipulation that I use it to produce livestock. And that I never sell the property."

"You said 'willed it.' Did they die?"

She winced as a pain of regret traveled through her. "Together. In a car accident."

"That's too bad. They must've thought a lot of you."

"They didn't have any children, and the three of us were always close. To be honest, I was shocked when I found out they'd left the place to me. They owned a little ranch of their own in the Prescott area, but I had no idea they owned land here in Nevada."

"So Prescott is where you're from originally?"

"No. I lived in Phoenix. But I spent every summer and weekend I could with my aunt and uncle. That's where I learned about horses and cattle. Uncle Rob had done that all his life. He taught me a lot."

"I see. So you decided to take on the challenge of turning the land here in Nevada into something."

Actually, she'd first thought of her move from Phoenix to Nevada as an escape, not a challenge. She'd wanted to get away from the crushing pain of her divorce and her clueless parents. But it hadn't taken long for her to begin to see the property as the future instead of a refuge.

"Something like that," she murmured.

He didn't say anything more. After a few moments passed, she looked over to see he'd closed his eyes and was once again resting his head against the back of the seat. No doubt his injury was causing him some misery. Talking probably made it worse.

That was okay with her. She'd already shared more about herself with this man in the past few minutes than she'd ever told anyone. What in the heck was that about? Since her brother, Andy, was killed five years ago, looking at any person wearing a law-enforcement badge had left her cold. So why was she spilling her personal life to this one? It didn't make sense. Except that he seemed different somehow from the cool, professional policemen who'd tried to explain away an eighteen-year-old's death.

Doing her best to shove the confusing doubts and questions from her mind, she concentrated on the traffic and hoped Evan didn't drift off to sleep before giving her directions to his home.

As if reading her thoughts, he suddenly spoke. "Before you get to the Washoe Lake turnoff, there's a gravel road that goes west. Take it. Three miles in, you'll see the entrance to the Silver Horn. Cross the cattle guard and stay on that road until you reach the ranch house."

"Got it."

Twenty minutes later, Noelle was wondering whether she'd made the correct turn a few miles back or she was driving them deeper into the wilderness. In the past half hour, the only thing she'd seen was a dark dirt road. But she was loath to wake her passenger and question him. He needed the rest. And the absence of his low, rich voice made it easier for her to keep her mind on driving.

Eventually, she spotted a cattle guard up ahead. As she drove closer, she could see it was flanked on either side with rock pillars. A sign that simply read Silver Horn swung from an arch of metal pipe spanning the entrance. She steered the truck over the metal ridges and hoped the ranch house wasn't far off.

Another fifteen minutes passed before Noelle finally caught a glimpse of lights on a far-off hill. When Evan had told her it was a long drive from town to his place, he hadn't been exaggerating. But that hardly mattered now. In a few minutes, she'd finally be rid of Detective Calhoun. The idea left her torn between extreme relief and unexplainable sadness.

Someone was beating the side of his head with a hammer. Evan fought as hard as he could to defend himself until the nightmare eventually had him bolting forward in the seat, causing the seat belt to latch tight against his throat.

"What the hell?" he muttered as he struggled to thrust the nylon strap away.

"You were having a dream. You're okay."

The feminine voice was strong and steady and enough to break through the last vestiges of the disturbing dream.

He opened his eyes and looked at her. Suddenly everything came rushing back to him. "Oh. It's you. Noelle."

"That's right. You've been asleep. But I think you're almost home now."

Wiping a hand over his eyes, he drew in a long breath and scooted up in the seat. Ahead of them, he could see the tall pines and poplar trees lining the driveway to the Silver Horn ranch house. For a few moments today, after Noelle had found him in the gulch, he'd wondered if he would ever see this place or his family again. But now that he realized he was going to live, he dreaded the berating he would surely get from his grandfather Bart Calhoun.

Realizing the truck was slowing, Evan glanced over to see Noelle gazing past the trees to the three-story brick house and the blaze of Christmas lights decorating its face, the lawn and the long walkway.

"This is where you live?"

"Ever since I was born," he answered easily. "Why? Is anything wrong?"

She turned her attention away from the house and back to the circular driveway. "No. I'm relieved that I didn't make a wrong turn and you're finally home."

He said, "Just park at the end of the sidewalk and I can make it the rest of the way."

She stopped the truck at the walk lined with low-growing juniper bushes. The evergreens were threaded with tiny, twinkling lights, turning the walkway into a dazzling trail.

"I'd be honored if you'd come in and meet my family," he said. "Greta, our cook, will have leftovers from dinner. After everything I've put you through today, you must be hungry."

Her tight hold on the steering wheel never lessened. "No thanks," she said bluntly. "I have to be getting home."

Even though the effort caused the gash in his head to hurt, he attempted to smile. "I promise I'm the only lawman that lives here. The rest make their living off cattle and horses."

Clearly not finding his remark amusing, she stared straight ahead. "I'm sure your folks are fine people. But I have chores waiting on me."

For some reason, the thought of her going back to that windswept hill and modest little house struck him hard. There wasn't much there but a barn full of hay, a handful of horses and a small herd of cattle. Why had she chosen such a hard, isolated life for herself? he wondered.

That's none of your business, Evan. And she clearly isn't about to let it become your business. So forget it and let her be on her way.

He reached over to shake her hand. She dropped the steering wheel long enough to oblige him. Her grip was strong, but brief.

"Well, thank you for all your trouble, Noelle. I can truly say I'd rather we met under different circumstances, but I'm very grateful you came along when you did."

"Forget it," she said curtly, then looked at him. "You never did say what you were doing out there riding in the hills. It had to be more than following four-wheeler tracks. Don't you think I have a right to know?"

"Actually, you should know. A few weeks ago, a body was discovered just a few miles from your place. I was following up on some leads regarding that case."

Her brows lifted slightly. "I read about it in the newspaper. But I didn't think it was that close—and the article didn't say anything about it being a homicide."

"I'm not saying it was a homicide, either. That detail hasn't been determined yet. But it's a fact that gangs sometimes meet out in the area not far from your property. To avoid the law coming down on them, we think. Have you ever seen anything suspicious? Especially around the dry gulch where you found me?"

"No. Never. Sometimes when the weather is nice, there might be a few teenagers sitting around smoking and drinking beer. Not far off the county road, on the property next to mine, there's a rock formation with a cave beneath. The kids use it as a place to hang out."

Feeling the need to caution her, he said, "Those might not be innocent teenagers, Noelle."

She turned a hard look on him. "I might've known you'd say something like that. A group of kids, cigarettes and beer. That instantly makes them gang members, thieves or murderers, doesn't it?"

There was more than sarcasm in her voice. There was downright anger. Her reaction made him wonder whether, as a teenager, she'd been targeted by the law. Though the notion hardly seemed likely, it was clear that something had hardened her toward police officers.

"No. I'm only saying it would be wise of you to use caution. A woman alone is—"

"No different than a man alone," she finished briskly. "Now, do you think you can get to the door under your own steam or do I need to help you?"

In his line of work, Evan was used to dealing with belligerent people. Some reacted out of fear, others out of downright meanness. No matter the reason, he'd been trained to keep his patience and let the barbs and jabs hit the invisible armor he always kept around him. But in Noelle's case, he found her unfounded resentment hard to take.

"I think I can manage," he said stiffly, then reached for his wallet. "Let me pay you for bringing me home and tending to my horse. I'd like to believe the rest of your help was a Good Samaritan act."

"I don't want your money. And as for being a Good Samaritan, I don't walk away from wounded animals. Or humans."

"Fine." He opened the truck door and climbed out. "Thanks again. Maybe we'll see each other again sometime. I know that would make you happy."

"Deliriously so," she muttered, her eyes focused on the windshield in front of her.

"Goodbye, Noelle."

She didn't reply, so he simply shut the door to the truck and started walking toward the house. But halfway there, he glanced over his shoulder at her disappearing taillights and wondered why it even mattered that she hadn't told him goodbye.

Chapter Three

During the long drive home, Noelle cried so hard the flood of tears made it difficult to see the road. She'd always prided herself on being emotionally stable. Not once since she'd moved to Nevada to start a new life had she shed a tear. Not for the death of her beloved aunt and uncle. Nor for the divorce, the break with her parents or even the loss of her brother. None of those things had melted her resolve to stay strong and in control.

So, damn it, why was she crying tonight? Why had a lawman with a lump on the side of his head and a goofy grin on his face turned her into a ball of jumbled emotions?

She was ashamed of herself for many reasons. If she was half the woman she wanted to believe she was, she would turn the truck around, drive back to that big mansion and apologize to the man. But tonight she was discovering she wasn't nearly as strong as she thought, and that jolted her. Whether he knew it or not, Evan Calhoun was forcing her to look at parts of herself she didn't want to see. Tonight or ever.

When she finally arrived home, she left her truck and walked straight to the barn. The horses were hanging their heads over the top rail of the corral, waiting impatiently for their supper. Earlier this evening, before she'd driven Evan to the emergency room, she'd turned his paint into the corral with her horses, and so far they weren't trying to kick or bite each other to death. Which was a relief. If his horse came up lame or injured while under her care, Evan's family would no doubt hold her responsible.

The fact that she'd asked him about selling the animal stung her cheeks with embarrassment. She'd recognized the horse was from good bloodstock, but she'd never imagined he'd come from a ranch like the Silver Horn. A horse of Lonesome's quality would carry a hefty price tag. One that would never fit into her budget.

At one time, she could've bought dozens of horses like the paint and never made a dent in her bank account. Money had been at her fingertips to buy anything she'd desired. But the cost of living the same sort of lifestyle as her parents had been too high for Noelle. Especially when she'd learned that her father, Neal, had earned a portion of his millions by not-so-honest business practices.

The best decision Noelle had ever made in her life was to turn her back on all that wealth, and the phoniness, and move here to Nevada. Even if it meant she ate canned tuna for dinner instead of beef steak and wore work boots instead of stilettos.

At the barn, she wasted no time pouring grain for the horses and filling their hay manger. The cow she'd penned next to the horses had been recuperating from a respiratory infection. Noelle injected her with a shot of antibiotics, then spread hay for her and the calf.

Once her chores at the barn were finished, she returned to the house and went straight to the bathroom to shower. It wasn't until she was standing in front of the vanity that she caught sight of her image in the medicine-chest mirror. The reflection shocked her. Her eyes were swollen, and tears had marked tracks down her dusty cheeks.

Disgusted by her unreasonable attitude toward Evan and her emotional breakdown, she pulled a washcloth from the vanity and stepped into the shower. But even after her face was drenched clean from the warm water, she still couldn't shake the memory of Evan's wounded expression.

He'd been not only offended by her sharp retorts but also hurt. Why had she said all that to him? Why had she deliberately set out to make him dislike her?

You know why, Noelle. Just when you'd started thinking he might be different, he'd talked about teenagers as if they were all potential criminals. He dug up those painful memories you've been trying so hard to bury. You might as well face it now. Evan Calhoun is no different from the officer who shot and killed Andy. And the sooner you realize that, the better off you'll be.

Trying to shut out the terrible voice in her head, Noelle finished her shower, then wrapped herself in a heavy robe and walked out to the kitchen to fix something to eat.

Tomorrow would be a new day, she told herself as she shoved a piece of bologna between two pieces of bread. And she was going to do her best to put this one behind her.

The next morning when Evan opened his eyes, he was shocked to see daylight seeping through the curtains and the digital clock on the nightstand clicking to 7:35.

He was going to be late for work!

He bolted upright in the bed before the ordeal of yesterday had time to creep into his sleep-fogged brain.

The sudden movement sent pain crashing from one side of his skull to the other, causing him to grab his head with both hands and curse.

"Oh, hell!"

Evan was still waiting for the ache to subside when a light knock sounded on the door, but he dared not go open it. Instead, he called in a strained voice, "Whoever you are, come in. Just walk softly."

The door creaked open, and a female voice spoke softly. "It's me, Tessa. Greta sent me up with your breakfast and a pain pill."

Evan wasn't at all sure he could eat. But since he'd not had a full meal since yesterday morning, he realized he needed to try.

He glanced at the tall, slender maid as she placed the breakfast tray on the nightstand. Even though she was barely out of her teens, she'd worked for the Calhoun family for a few years now. Evan thought of her as a sister more than anything and treated her as such.

"I fell asleep last night before remembering to set my alarm," he mumbled. "Why didn't someone wake me? I'm going to be late for work."

Tessa eyed him with disbelief. "You're not going to work today. Didn't you read the orders the doctor sent home with you?"

Read? After listening to Grandfather Bart rake him over the coals for allowing a horse to dump him, Evan had done well to make it upstairs and fall into bed.

"I don't care what those orders say. As soon as I eat and shower, I'm going to the office."

She handed him a thin china cup balanced on a matching saucer. "You feel that good?"

Even though he felt as if an earthquake was rattling his insides, he managed to take the coffee without spilling it. "No. I feel like hell. But the office is overloaded with cases right now."

Tessa walked across the room and pulled back the drapes to reveal a view of the distant mountains covered with tall evergreens. Silver Horn land went beyond those mountains to the west and across the desert hills to the east. Thousands of acres belonged to one family. His family. The fact would probably be mind-boggling to a woman like Noelle, who was trying to eke out a living with the barest necessities.

Dear God, he didn't need to be thinking about her and her smart mouth. It would only make his head hurt worse. But even with the pain crowding every bit of space inside his skull, she'd managed to find room enough to insert herself.

"Tessa, would you like living on an isolated ranch alone?"

The young woman paused and looked at him with a puzzled expression. "No. Why? Am I going to be transferred to a line shack or something?"

He laughed and immediately regretted it as shards of pain splintered the left side of his head. "Not hardly. We couldn't do without you. I was just wondering. I met someone yesterday who…puzzled me."

Tessa gave him an understanding smile. "I meet people like that every day. And then I remind myself that I can't expect everyone to be like me. We all want different things. That's what makes each of us interesting, don't you think?"

Ignoring the food on the tray, Evan reached for the pain reliever and swallowed it with a swig of coffee. "You're too smart to be nineteen," he told her.

Lifting her chin, she started toward the door. "You

know very well that I'm twenty-one. And eat your breakfast before it gets cold."

Fifteen minutes later, Evan felt human enough to follow Tessa's suggestion. By then the food was cold, but that didn't matter. The eggs and bacon would ease the gnawing in his stomach.

He'd finished the meal and was swinging his legs over the edge of the bed when a hard rap sounded at the door and Finn stepped into the room. His younger brother was a lanky, good-looking guy with curly auburn hair that was usually hidden beneath a gray cowboy hat. At twenty-eight, he'd been manager of the horse division of the ranch for four years. It was a job that kept him going from daylight to dark and beyond.

"What are you doing in the house at this hour?" Evan asked.

Finn walked over to the tray on the nightstand and plucked up a piece of half-eaten toast. "I've already been down to the barns. I came back to check on you. Dad tells me that Lonesome dumped you. That horse has never bucked in his life. What happened?"

Evan frowned. "He didn't buck yesterday. A bird flew up in his face and scared him. He sort of reared up and jumped sideways at the same time. I wasn't expecting it and fell off. That's all. And before you start in on me, I know I should keep up my riding skills, but it's not like I have the time."

"I'm not going to preach. Even the best of us can lose our seat from time to time." Munching the toast, Finn leaned down to inspect the gash on Evan's head. "That looks nasty. How do you feel this morning?"

"Okay. Just a little headache," Evan lied.

Finn looked relieved. "Good. When Dad said you had a concussion—well, the whole family and I couldn't help thinking about Mom. Are you sure the doctor looked you over good?"

"Finn, they took so many scans and X-rays of my head yesterday, you could stand me out in the yard tonight and use me as a Christmas light. Thanks for worrying about me, though."

Finn laid a hand on his shoulder. "We love you. That's all," he said, then turned and started toward the door. "You need anything? I'll tell Tessa to bring it up."

What he needed most was to get one tall cowgirl out of his head. "No thanks. But wait a minute, Finn. About Lonesome, he's—"

Finn turned back to him. "Yeah. I've already heard. You left him at the house of the woman who found you. I believe Dad said her name was Barnes. Is that right?"

"Noelle Barnes. She lives on a small spread over by Douglas County."

"Okay. Give me the directions to her place and I'll have one of the hands pick him up today and pay her for her trouble."

"No. Don't offer her money. I've already tried that. I…" Evan broke off, shocked to feel his face getting hot. Maybe, if he was lucky, Finn would put the flush down to the three cups of coffee he'd swallowed with his breakfast. "I wanted to see if you could do without the horse for a while. Just leave him there. As a favor to me."

Finn frowned with confusion. "What?"

Evan blew out a frustrated breath. "The woman—she took a liking to Lonesome and wanted to know if the ranch would sell him to her. But, Finn, I doubt she has two pennies to rub together, and she's not the sort to accept charity. I thought maybe we could simply forget to pick up the horse."

An understanding grin suddenly spread across Finn's face. "Look, as far as I'm concerned, the woman rescued you from a bad situation. I'd be glad to give her two or three horses for saving your life."

"One will be sufficient."

"Fine. We'll leave Lonesome where he is. And if anyone asks about him, I'll just say he found a new home."

"You're the best, brother."

Waving away his thanks, Finn left the room. Evan rose shakily to his feet. Doctor's orders or not, he had to get back to work and focus his mind on solving crimes instead of a barbed-tongued woman with velvety brown eyes.

Nearly a week later, Noelle drove into town for a load of feed and stopped on her way out at the Grubstake Café for coffee and a fat cinnamon roll that was a specialty of the old diner.

Even at nine in the morning, the large rustic room was still full of breakfast diners and coffee drinkers. Noelle took a seat at the long wooden bar and looked around the old eating place.

Since she'd been here last, someone had put up a blue spruce in the far corner of the room and decorated it with lights, candy canes and silver tinsel. Overhead, huge ornaments hung from the rafters, while Christmas music played from a nearby radio.

It was the time of year for celebrations, gift giving and family gatherings. Noelle would participate in none of that. She would, however, put up a small tree in her house and give her livestock an extra helping of feed on Christmas Day.

Through the years, when her aunt Geneva and uncle Rob had been alive, she'd spent wonderful holidays with them on their ranch near Prescott. Her aunt had always cooked for days before the event, and her uncle had decorated the house and lawn and even the barns with lights and evergreen branches. On Christmas Eve, they had attended church services. The next morning, they sat around the tree and opened simple but meaningful gifts.

Noelle's mother and father had never understood why their daughter hadn't wanted to travel with them to some exotic island or exciting city to celebrate the Christmas season. They'd not understood that their children hadn't wanted extravagant vacations for a gift. They'd simply wanted their parents to be home and attentive. But that scenario wasn't Neal and Maxine's style. As a result, Noelle had always chosen to go to her aunt and uncle's, while teenage Andy had spent his Christmases with one of his grungy friends.

"Noelle, has anyone waited on you yet?"

At the sound of Jessi's voice, Noelle looked up at the redheaded waitress standing directly behind the bar. The young woman was one of the few friends Noelle had made since she'd moved to the Carson City area. "Not yet."

Resting a pencil over her ear, Jessi leaned forward and said under her breath, "We got new help and she's as slow as molasses. But she's so nice, I can't help but like her."

Smiling vaguely, Noelle shook her head. "Have patience. She'll get into the swing of things. And I'm in no hurry. All I need is coffee and a cinnamon roll."

"Coming right up," Jessi told her.

When the waitress returned a few moments later with the order, she placed it in front of Noelle and added a small box next to the plate.

Surprised, Noelle stared at the gift wrapped in bright red-and-green paper. "What is this?"

Grinning impishly, Jessi shrugged. "Just a little something from me. You always give me tips when I know you can't afford them. That means a lot to me. Open it."

"It's still a while before Christmas," Noelle pointed out.

"So it's a few days. We're supposed to give to our friends all through the year."

Since Jessi wasn't about to let her take the gift without opening it, Noelle quickly tore off the festive paper and lifted the lid on a white cardboard box. Nestled in a bed of cotton was a barrette covered with colored rhinestones. It was feminine and sparkly and something that she would've never splurged on for herself.

"Oh, it's lovely, Jessi." For the second time in a matter of days, tears filled Noelle's eyes. Feeling foolishly emotional, she tried to blink them away. "You shouldn't have done this."

"Don't be silly. It didn't cost much."

Noelle gazed at the hair jewelry and couldn't help but remember one particular Christmas Eve. It was Noelle's birthday and since her parents had rarely acknowledged the day separately from Christmas, she'd been hopeful when they'd given her a gift to open early that whatever was inside the box was just for her special day. But then she quickly learned that the matching barrettes covered with real diamonds and emeralds had been purposely given to her to wear to a Christmas Eve party the family was planning to attend. Those barrettes hadn't been given with the same sincerity as this gift from Jessi. That made all the difference to Noelle.

"I realize that," Noelle said in a husky voice, "but you need to watch your pennies, too."

Jessi laughed. "It's just money. And I think it's high time I saw you in something pretty."

Before Noelle could thank her properly, a diner at the end of the bar called to Jessi. The young woman hurried away to tend to the customer.

Noelle put the lid back on the box and was digging into the cinnamon roll when someone sat down on the stool next to her. Always one to keep to herself, she didn't bother looking around until the man spoke in a deep, familiar voice.

"This is a surprise," he said. "I've never seen you in here before."

Evan Calhoun! How had she managed to come across him here in the Grubstake this morning? Some sort of crazy fate was throwing them together.

Turning her head in his direction, she said, "I've never seen you here, either. But I don't drop by that often. Maybe once a week in the midmorning."

"Oh. I usually come in every day before duty."

His gaze roamed over her face and Noelle had never been more aware of her appearance. Although she hadn't taken great pains when she'd dressed that morning to come to town, she had put on a nice black sweater with her jeans and dabbed a bit of pink color on her cheeks and lips. Was he noticing that? Or trying to figure out some way to insult her as she'd insulted him the other night? Either notion made her cringe inwardly.

Trying to clear away the tightness in her throat, she asked, "How's the head?"

"Back to normal. Thanks for asking."

Drawing in a deep, bracing breath, she stared at the half-eaten sweet roll. "I—uh—hadn't expected to see you again, but now I'm glad I ran into you like this. It gives me the opportunity to apologize to you. I behaved rudely the other night, and I regret it. You didn't deserve that from me."

She could sense him looking at her, yet she didn't have the courage to turn and face him. Something about his eyes made her feel as though he was looking right into the deepest part of her, and that was a place she definitely didn't want him to see.

"We'd both had a tough day," he replied. "As far as I'm concerned, all's forgotten."

"That's kind of you."

She lifted the thick coffee mug to her lips. While she sipped, Jessi returned to take Evan's order.

"Coffee and one of those things that Noelle's eating," he told the waitress.

Surprised, Jessi glanced at the both of them. "I wasn't aware that you two knew each other."

Evan smiled. "Noelle saved my life a few days ago."

Noelle spluttered with embarrassment, and Jessi leaned curiously over the bar toward Evan. "Really? You're the lawman. Aren't you supposed to be the one saving the lives around here?"

He laughed. "The tables were turned this time."

Groaning, Noelle said, "It was no big thing, Jessi. Evan fell off his horse and I just happened to help him get home. That's all."

The waitress was clearly disappointed. "Oh. And here I was thinking I would hear about you collaring some criminal."

To Noelle's relief, Jessi was called away at that moment. She used the distraction to turn her attention back to the last of the sweet roll.

Evan said, "I hope Lonesome isn't giving you any problems."

She glanced over at him. This time she allowed herself to take note of his clean-shaven face, the brown leather jacket covering a white shirt and the pistol holstered at his side. He looked strong and in total control today, and she had to admit to herself that he was too damned attractive to be walking safely among the female population.

"So you're aware he's still at my place?"

"Uh, yes. My brother Finn is in charge of all the Silver Horn horses, and he let me know it might be some time before he could send a hand out to pick up the paint."

She frowned. His excuse hardly made sense, especially when a ranch as big as the Silver Horn probably had dozens of hired hands. "Then I could deliver him. It wouldn't be that big of a problem."

"Oh, no. I mean, there's no urgency about it. The ranch hands have more than enough horses to ride. Just keep Lonesome there and use him like he's yours. He'll be needing some exercise anyway."

"I wouldn't want to do that. If he came up lame, I'd be responsible."

"We have a vet on the ranch. If that ever happened, he'd deal with the problem. In the meantime, just take good care of Lonesome until someone eventually comes around to pick him up."

Seeing she couldn't argue with him, she simply shrugged her acquiescence. "Okay. I'll be glad to."

Jessi returned with Evan's coffee and roll. As he began to eat, Noelle placed a tip by her empty plate and rose to her feet.

As she picked up the little box containing her Christmas gift, he asked, "You're not leaving, are you?"

"Yes. I need to get home and unload the feed before it starts to snow."

He glanced over his shoulder and looked out the window at the parking lot. "That's your truck? The black one with the feed sacks stacked in the back?"

"That's it," she answered. "Guess you were too groggy the other day to remember it."

Dismayed, he turned back to her. "You're not going to unload all of that by yourself, are you?"

She smiled vaguely. "Like I told you, I take care of the ranch by myself. I'm strong. Lifting a fifty-pound feed sack is nothing new to me."

His appreciative gaze traveled over her. "Then the other day in the gulch, you probably could've slung me over the saddle."

"I'm not so sure. But I would've certainly tried." She turned to leave. "Goodbye, Evan."

Before she could step away from the bar, he caught her arm. "Please. Wait a minute," he said. "I have something to ask you."

Curious, she eased back onto the stool. "About Lonesome?"

"No. I'm not worried about him. He's in good hands." He released his hold on her arm, even while his gaze held fast to hers. "I was wondering—do you have anything pressing to do tomorrow?"

His question caught her completely off guard. Instead of being able to think quickly and give him a resounding yes, she paused too long to make anything sound convincing. "Not exactly. Just routine chores."

"How would you like to take a drive with me up to Virginia City? My maternal grandparents, Tuck and

Alice Reeves, live close to there, and I've been promising them a visit. Tomorrow is the only day off I'm going to have for a while."

The invitation stunned her. She had been rude to this man, and the two of them were barely acquainted. "Why would you want to take a stranger with you to visit your grandparents?"

He smiled at her and as Noelle's gaze followed the line of his white teeth, she inwardly shivered. The mere idea of being close to this man shook her senses. Behind that incredibly masculine face and rock-hard body, he was a lawman. How could she be attracted to him?

She couldn't answer that. She only knew that for the first time in years, she remembered that she was a woman. And the feeling was too good to pass up.

"Oh, I think I'll be safe in your company," he said with a lazy grin. "And I thought you might enjoy seeing something other than that little ranch of yours. Just in case you're wondering, my grandparents love having company. You'd be very welcome."

Since she'd moved to the Carson City area, she'd been asked out on a few dates by men she'd met through connections to her work. She'd refused all of them. And something told her if she was smart now, she'd give Evan Calhoun a loud, decisive no.

But something strange was going on inside her. For the life of her she couldn't seem to form the word, much less say it to the man.

"Actually, it might be nice to see Virginia City," she said before she could stop herself. "I've never driven up that far north."

Before she could guess his intentions, he reached for her hand and clasped it tightly between both of his.

"Great. I'll drive out to your place and pick you up in the morning. Is ten okay?"

Across the room, she spotted Jessi staring curiously at the two of them. Noelle wondered whether the heat from Evan's hands was racing straight to her cheeks and staining them red. They definitely felt as if they'd turned a hot scarlet.

"Ten is fine." She awkwardly eased her hand from his. "I'll see you then."

He lifted a hand in farewell, and Noelle left the café.

On the drive home, she tried to think of anything and everything besides Evan Calhoun. She had a whole list of chores to be finished before nightfall. She didn't have time to daydream about a man. Any man, she told herself.

But a half hour later, she was home and changing out of her sweater and boots when it dawned on her that she'd been so shaken by Evan's invitation, she'd forgotten to pay the ticket for the coffee and cinnamon roll.

Feeling worse than sappy, she picked up the phone and punched in the number for the café. Thankfully, Jessi answered.

"It's Noelle," she told the waitress. "I don't know if you've noticed yet, but I forgot and left the café without paying my bill. Can you take care of it for me until I come back in?"

"Don't worry. I've already taken care of it," Jessi assured her. "But I would like to know what's going on with you. Evan Calhoun was holding your hand! What was that all about?"

Noelle drew in a shaky breath, then blew it out. "I'm

not sure, Jessi. I think I might've just made the biggest mistake in my life."

Either that or she was finally waking up from a long, cold sleep.

Chapter Four

The next morning, when Evan arrived at Noelle's lonely little ranch a few minutes before ten, he realized just how loopy he'd been the day he'd hit his head in the gulch. Everything he'd remembered about the place was like a foggy dream. Now, as he parked the truck a few yards away from the house, everything was crystal clear. Almost brutally so.

Even in his dazed state that day, he'd noticed the small size of the house. But he didn't recall it being this little, or the chipping stucco and weather-bleached trim so worn and in need of repair. Except for two small windows, the front of the dwelling was bare, with no sort of porch to shield the entrance. A stone positioned below the simple door acted as a step. Beyond the house, he could see a partial view of the old board barn. The whole structure was listing slightly to the east, as though it had grown tired of battling the years of westerly winds. But since the barn was in no danger of collapsing, Evan supposed it was serving its purpose.

As he walked to the door of the house, Evan couldn't help but think back to when he'd asked Tessa about living on an isolated ranch and she'd humorously asked if the family was going to send her to take care of a line shack. Evan had laughed at her question. But now, as he took a good look at Noelle's home, he realized that some of the line shacks on the Silver Horn were far sturdier and more comfortable. And though it shouldn't have, the fact made him feel a bit guilty about the wealth he'd been born into.

Noelle answered his knock fairly quickly. As soon as Evan took one look at her, he realized why he'd taken the trouble to ask her out. A pair of cream-colored jeans clung to her shapely hips and long legs, then finally disappeared into a pair of brown suede dress boots. A pumpkin-colored blouse caressed the fullness of her breasts and brought out the rich, russet highlights in her long, brown hair. Yet it was the strength of her features and the candor in her dark brown eyes that struck him the most.

"Good morning," she said. "Please come in while I finish gathering my things."

He stepped past her and directly into the cozy living room. Along the way, he caught the same flowery scent she'd been wearing the day he'd fallen off Lonesome. Damn. There were bits and pieces of that day he couldn't recall at all. Yet he could remember very distinctly how this woman had looked and smelled. He supposed with only a part of his brain working, the male instinct had taken over.

"It looks like we're going to have a beautiful day today," he told her. "I hope the weather holds. I'd like to show you around my grandparents' place without freezing you."

"I'm outdoors every day, Evan. Rain or shine. Heat or cold. I'm used to it." Smiling faintly, she gestured toward the couch. "Have a seat if you like. I'll be only a minute."

She disappeared into another part of the house. Rather than taking a seat, Evan stood where he was and took a visual survey of the small room. The walls were painted a pale beige and covered with an assortment of prints, mostly outdoor scenes full of horses and Western landscapes. Linoleum covered the floor, and in places the brown-and-gold pattern was worn through to the black backing, but she'd hidden most of it with a braided rug in the center.

Along with the red couch he'd rested on the other day, there was a stuffed red armchair, both of which had faded to the color of a half-ripened watermelon. A wooden rocker with a thin pad tied to the seat was jammed in one corner, while directly across from it was a small television set equipped with a pair of rabbit ears. Without a proper antenna, he doubted she received enough signal to get the public-access channel out of Carson City, much less a regular station with nationwide programming.

Did she live in this manner because she was frugal, he wondered, or simply because she lacked the funds to do better? Either way, he was more than intrigued by the woman. Yet the lifestyle she'd chosen was her business, and she'd already made it fairly clear that she didn't want him poking his nose in it.

The sound of her footsteps had him turning to see her stepping through the open doorway. A gray woolen coat was thrown over her arm, while a brown leather purse swung from her shoulder.

"Will I need anything other than my coat and purse?"

"Not a thing," he said with a smile. "Do you have the barn situated like you need it? The horses—"

"Yes. Everything will be fine until this evening."

"Good. Then let's get going. If we're lucky, Grandmother will have something cooking on the stove."

He followed her out of the house, then stepped to one

side while he waited for her to lock the door. But she didn't. When she started toward his truck, Evan stared after her in dismay.

"Noelle? You forgot to lock the house."

Glancing over her shoulder at him, she shook her head. "I didn't forget. I never lock it."

Stunned, Evan quickly caught up to her. "Never lock it? But someone could walk in and steal anything they wanted!"

She shot him a bored look. "And just what would they be getting, Mr. Detective? A few pieces of clothing? Some mismatched dishes? A little trinket box full of costume jewelry? A TV set that you'd do well to sell at a pawnshop for twenty-five dollars? No. If someone wants to get in the house that badly, I'd rather them walk through the door instead of breaking out the windows."

Her logic set him back on his heels. For a moment, he wasn't sure how to reply. Her reasoning made sense, and it pointed out just how few material things she owned.

"What about Christmas gifts?" he asked. "At this time of year, if you have any of those hidden away—"

"No," she interrupted him. "I don't really do much in the way of Christmas buying."

He wondered whether her finances didn't allow for shopping or she simply didn't enjoy the holiday. Either way, now wasn't the time to ask.

Taking her by the arm, he urged her on to the truck. Along the way, he said, "As an officer of the law, I tell folks all the time not to make it easy for thieves to steal or commit a crime. But—and don't ever repeat this to Sheriff Wainwright—in your case, I can see your point."

As he opened the truck door to help her into the cab,

she actually gave him a broad smile. "You can? That's surprising."

He chuckled. "I can have an open mind. When I really work at it."

Minutes later, after they'd driven away from her place, Noelle glanced around the plush interior of the truck, then allowed her gaze to settle on Evan. Although he was dressed casually in faded jeans and a denim jacket over a green paisley shirt, he wore the clothes with an easy air that could only come from a wealth of self-confidence. And though she hated to admit it, the attitude added volumes to his sexy appearance.

They'd traveled a few miles in companionable silence when she asked, "What made you want to become a lawman?"

With his brows pulled together, he darted her a glance. "You make it sound like I've chosen to have an incurable disease."

She could've told him that for the past five years, she'd considered lawmen as loathsome as an incurable disease, but this man was going out of his way to repay her for a kind deed. For today she would try to forget that he wore a pistol on his hip and a badge on his chest.

"Sorry," she said. "It's hard for me to figure you out. I mean, your family owns and runs a huge ranch. You had other options and directions you could've taken in your life. Instead, you chose to be an officer of the law."

He stared thoughtfully ahead at the lonesome two-lane highway. "You're right. I grew up learning all about raising cattle and horses and the round-the-clock work it takes to run a place the size of the Horn. My dad even says I'm good at ranching, and maybe I am. But I had other interests, too." Glancing at her again, he said,

"To answer your question better, it was my granddad Tuck, the one you'll meet today, who directed me toward being a law officer."

"Oh. So I take it he's not a rancher."

"No. Not like the Calhoun family. Granddad runs a few head of cows and has a couple of horses, but he doesn't do it for a living. Having livestock around is just something to give him a reason to get outdoors and stay busy. And keep out of Grandmother's hair. You see, he's a retired sheriff."

Dear Lord, somehow she'd managed to land herself smack in the middle of a family of lawmen! What had she done to deserve a bunch of sad reminders shoved at her? Why couldn't she have found an old, wrinkled rancher in the gulch that day? A bent, bowlegged cowboy who had simply ridden off his range and gotten lost? Instead, she'd found a hunky deputy who happened to be a member of one of the richest families in the state.

"Oh," she said. "Did he work for the same office you do now?"

"No. He was the sheriff of Storey County for more than twenty years. A damned good one, I might add."

Twenty years. That wasn't just being a lawman, she thought. That was devoting your life to the job.

"Apparently, he was revered," she agreed. "Or the public wouldn't have continued to reelect him."

"Granddad had been in office for only a few years when a pair of fugitives shot and killed a Nevada highway patrolman down in the southern part of the state. The two headed north in an attempt to escape and eventually ditched their vehicle and made a run into the mountains. I was fourteen at the time, and when Granddad went after them, I was terrified that he was going to be shot and killed. Instead, he brought the men back to town in cuffs. That's when I knew I wanted to be a lawman. I wanted to bring mean people to justice and keep innocent ones from being hurt."

Noelle looked at him and tried to imagine him as a young teenager, frightened for the safety of his grandfather. And for the first time since Andy had died, she thought about the fears and sacrifices that families of law officials went through on a daily basis. If Evan ever took a wife, would she worry that each day he went to work might be the last time she would ever see him? It was a jolting possibility. One that Noelle didn't want to contemplate.

Swallowing at the unexpected tightness in her throat, she said, "Your grandfather must have been the town hero after that."

"Granddad Tuck never was one to take credit for any accomplishments made by his office. Over the years, he's done plenty of heroic deeds, but Granddad never wanted anyone to think of him in those terms. He says a person who's just doing a job isn't a hero."

She studied Evan for long, thoughtful moments as more and more questions about this man began to prod and push her to say things she'd normally keep to herself. "So you wanted to be like your granddad."

A wry grin slanted his lips. "I never believed I could be as good a lawman as Granddad, but I wanted to try. All he ever wanted was to help and protect people, and that's all I want to do."

Help and protect. A part of her understood and appreciated the good services that law officers provided a community. Rules had to be followed, and someone had to enforce them. She even understood they performed a dangerous and thankless job. But there was another part of her that couldn't forget the image of her brother's coffin being lowered into the ground. And no one had been held accountable for his death. As though Andy had meant nothing.

Yet here she was on a date of sorts with a deputy sheriff, one who was a detective, at that. What was wrong with her, anyway? It was as if she was the one who'd fallen off her horse and knocked her head instead of Evan. But something about him made her almost forget he was a lawman, something that made her want to learn the kind of man he was when he wasn't wearing his badge. What made him laugh or growl with anger? Did he ever dream of love and marriage and children? Or was the law more than enough to fill his life?

A mile or two had passed before she pushed the questions out of her mind and simply asked, "Do you see your grandparents often?"

"Not as much as I'd like. The opportunity to take a whole day off doesn't come up very often. Most of the time, we have more cases than we have detectives. When I do get a break, I usually have other obligations. While I take a breather today, my partner is working on our most pressing case, the body found in your area of the county." He glanced over at her. "What about you? Do you travel much?"

She shook her head. "Never. Since I moved up here to Nevada, I haven't traveled anywhere. It's been four years."

"Somehow that doesn't surprise me."

Frowning slightly, she looked at him. "What does that mean?"

"It just means that you don't seem like the traveling sort. You're more of the stay-at-home type. Am I right?"

Damn, this man seemed to have a knack for summing her up and getting it right. He was also making Noelle realize things about herself that she'd never thought about before. Like how much she'd isolated herself on the ranch since she'd come to Nevada.

"You are right," she admitted. "I like the quiet."

You like hiding, too. Because you don't have the courage to step back into the land of the living. Because you don't want to give yourself the chance to meet a man you could love and build a future with.

Hating the little mocking voice in her head, she did her best to silence it, while across the seat, Evan grinned, totally unaware that he was shaking up her senses in ways that they'd never been shaken before.

"Well, my grandparents aren't exactly the quiet sort," he said. "They're always doing something. I hope you'll like them."

Relieved that he hadn't followed up on her remark with a more personal question, she smiled back at him. "I'm looking forward to meeting them."

For the next half hour, they passed through bald hills covered with boulders, sagebrush and tall tufts of dead grass. In places, granite cliffs had been carved by the relentless weather, while in others, low, scrubby evergreens dotted the loamy soil. At one point, a large herd of mule deer was grazing off to the west of the highway, and Evan slowed the truck to give Noelle a better look at the wildlife.

Bending forward in the seat, she peered out the driver's window. "They're beautiful," she said softly. "In fact, this whole area is lovely. I'm glad you took me on this route."

Evan couldn't help but notice how the gentle appreciation on her face softened her features. Somewhere, beneath all the toughness she'd displayed that day in the gulch, was a sweet, feminine woman. And he was going to do his best to peel away the protective layers until he found her. But then what? Would he find that Noelle was a woman he could get serious about? He didn't yet know the answers to those questions. And he wasn't about to ruin the day by dwelling on them.

"Have you ever been to Washoe Lake?" he asked.

She straightened in her seat, and Evan immediately missed the sweet, flowery scent of her skin. "No. Never had any reason to go there."

He grunted with amusement. "You need a reason?"

She shrugged. "Well, fuel is expensive. And I don't have time for sightseeing. Besides, it would seem kind of silly, driving around by myself and looking at things just to be looking."

"Hmm. Are you always so practical?"

Out of the corner of his eye, he could see her frowning. He figured it had been a long time since anyone had taken the time or effort to bother her about anything.

She asked, "Do you always pester people with so many questions?"

He chuckled. "I'm a detective. How else am I going to get to the truth?"

Her frown deepened. "The truth? I'm not hiding anything."

He cast a pointed smile at her. "We all hide things, Noelle. Some of us just hide them deeper than others."

Fifteen minutes later, they passed through the tiny mining town of Silver City. Four miles north, they entered Virginia City. Since Noelle had confessed to him that she'd never visited the town before, he drove slowly through the main drag and pointed out a few historic spots.

"Back in the eighteen hundreds, during its mining heyday, this old town was wiped out by fire at least four or five times. I suppose it survived because there were enough folks determined to stick around and rebuild no matter what," he told her.

"I'd say that was determination," she replied as she gazed out at the board sidewalks and quaint little shops mostly catering to the flocks of tourists that visited each year. "Must have been something around here that made them want to risk everything to stay," she commented.

Signs of Christmas were everywhere, from the angels and stars hanging from the streetlamps to the twinkling lights and decorated trees in the store windows. For Evan, it was the time of year when he and his brothers were drawn even closer together. His home on the Silver Horn was adorned with decorations, the kitchen was full of rich food, and in the family room, gifts were piled high beneath a dazzling twelve-foot fir tree.

But not everyone was as lucky as he was, Evan thought. His line of work never failed to show him the ugly side of the season, when added stresses and strained finances caused abusive explosions in families, and thieves took advantage of the blessed holiday to steal a child's Christmas dreams.

"The something that held most folks around here was gold and silver," he said wryly.

"Well, the desert mountains are charming. I like it here. I might have wanted to stay, too, if I'd sunk my roots here first."

Intrigued by her comment, Evan glanced over at her profile. Because her attention was on the town, he had a chance to study the lovely line of her throat and the way her stubborn little chin curved into a pair of full, dusky pink lips.

The more time he spent with the woman, the more he wanted to know about her. But Evan had learned that patience was the key to gathering information. And he'd already decided that questioning this woman outright wasn't going to produce many answers. It would have to be her own idea to open up and really talk to him.

"Actually, Granddad Tuck was born on the place where he and Grandmother live now," he told her. "A midwife delivered him during a raging blizzard. My great-grandparents lived too far out of town to make it to Virginia City and the doctor. So I guess you could say his roots are deep in these mountains."

She looked at him, and Evan was struck by the faint melancholy shadows in her eyes.

"That must be very nice," she said. "When I was a young girl, I never knew whether my parents would stay in one place for long. I think that's one of the reasons I preferred to stay with my aunt and uncle. They had roots, and I always knew they'd be in the same place if I needed them. The same house. That was comforting to me."

Without needing to ask, Evan understood she was speaking of the aunt and uncle who'd willed her the little ranch she lived on now. When she spoke of them, there was warm affection in her voice, along with a sense of loss.

"Change can be upsetting," he said. "I think that's part of the reason why Grandfather Bart never wanted me to be a lawman. He didn't want anyone in his family to change—to be something different. When he first learned I was going to college in law enforcement, he had a walleyed fit. And later, after I went to work for the sheriff's office, he argued and demanded that I quit. He even tried to bribe me with money, vehicles—anything he thought might sway me to his way of thinking. He couldn't get it through his head that all I wanted was to wear a badge and enforce the law."

As the last of the town appeared in the rearview mirror, he could feel her curious gaze on the side of his face. It left him feeling warm and strange, as though she was seeing parts of him that no one else had ever seen before.

"So you and your paternal grandfather don't see eye to eye," she said thoughtfully. "Do your brothers get along with him?"

"For the most part. Clancy—he's the oldest—gets on well with Grandfather. So does Rafe. He's the middle of the five brothers, the ranch foreman. Finn—he's younger than Rafe—is over the horses. His relationship with Grandfather is strained at times, but they usually get along. As for our little Bowie, it's hard to say. He's been away in the marines for so long now, I honestly don't know how the two of them would get on if they were together for more than a day at a time."

"Oh. You have a brother in the military. So you're not the only one who strayed from ranching."

"No. And believe me, Grandfather Bart didn't like Bowie's choice of profession, either. But there wasn't much he could do about it." Evan gestured toward the stand of mountains in the near distance. "That's where we're going. It won't be long now."

Minutes later, the landscape began to change from bald desert mountains to those covered with tall evergreens. Along the foothills, enormous cottonwoods were now bare limbed, but in the summer, the trees shaded smaller willows and blooming sage. Evan had been over this road more times than he could count, and each time, he felt a sense of homecoming. Maybe that was because, like Noelle and her aunt and uncle, he'd always known his grandparents would be in the same place, the same house, waiting with open and loving arms.

As a child of socialite parents, Noelle had met all sorts of people in all types of places. The idea of being introduced to strangers had never made her nervous or doubtful about her appearance or conversation skills. But something about meeting Evan's grandparents was making her anxious. She'd met Evan only a few days ago. What were they going to think about him bringing her into their home? They might even get the idea that she'd jumped at the chance to snare a rich man. And telling them that she'd already gotten rid of one rich husband would be even more awkward.

Noelle was trying to convince herself that she had nothing to worry about when the truck rounded a deep curve and the Reeves home came into view. A two-story farmhouse nestled at the foot of a mountain in a copse of bare cottonwoods. The frame structure was painted a pale green, while the gingerbread trim was a darker hunter-green.

Evan drove down the short gravel drive to the house, and Noelle spotted a Nativity scene out on the lawn. As they drew closer, the beauty of the little stable with the animals gathered around it caught Noelle's complete attention.

"Oh, how lovely," she murmured. "I can't remember the last time I saw a Nativity scene with the shepherds and animals and all the wise men! And the little lean-to stable is made of real wooden boards!"

"Granddad will be happy to hear how much you appreciate the scene. It's something he's worked on for a long time. He made the stable first and then the manger holding baby Jesus. After that, each year he kept adding a piece or two. He had trouble finding just the right camel he wanted, though. Eventually, he located one in a town down in southern California, then drove all the way over there to collect it. He didn't trust a freight truck to get the camel safely up here to him."

This from a man who'd spent years of his life as a sheriff? The notion struck a spot so deep in Noelle that she felt a little dazed. Her own father had never lifted a finger to decorate anything for Christmas. If he had, things might have been a whole lot different for their family, she couldn't help thinking.

"Your granddad obviously put in a lot of work to build the Nativity scene."

"Believe me, Noelle, for him it was a labor of love."

A labor of love. Yes, it was obvious that Tuck Reeves was a man full of love. But as a sheriff had he ever made mistakes, she wondered, and hurt an innocent person?

Everyone makes mistakes, Noelle. You've made plenty of them. And you're making a mistake right now by trying to judge a man before you even meet him. Just like you were judging Evan that day in the gulch when he flashed his badge at you.

Noelle was listening so intently to the mocking voice in her head that Evan was already parking the truck behind a pair of vehicles in an open carport before she noticed the vehicle had come to a stop.

As he shut off the engine and removed his seat belt, he said, "Now that we're on the subject of Christmas, I've been wondering if you were named for the holiday. Or was Noelle just a name your parents liked?"

Surprised that he'd even made the connection, she looked at him. "Actually, I was born on Christmas Eve.

My mother wanted to name me Holly, but Dad took one look at me and decided Noelle was a better fit for his newborn daughter."

One corner of his mouth curved upward in a smile as his gaze slipped over her face. "Your dad was right. Noelle fits you perfectly. So your birthday is coming up soon. How are you going to celebrate it?"

The glint she spotted in his green eyes warmed her cheeks. "I won't be celebrating. It's just another day."

"That's awful."

Each year since she'd moved to Nevada, she'd received birthday cards from her parents, but for Noelle, the acknowledgments had seemed too little, too late. Now her birthday was a reminder that she no longer had a family. "I've never celebrated my birthday very much," she tried to explain. "It was always so close to Christmas that my family usually overlooked it and just let Christmas gifts do for both days."

He shook his head. "Well, maybe this year will be different," he said, then gave her a little grin. "Ready to go in?"

"Sure. If the inside of the house is decorated anything like the outside, I can't wait to see it."

He smiled. "Don't worry. There will be plenty inside for you to see. Whenever it comes to the holidays, my grandparents are like two little kids."

He climbed out of the truck. While he skirted the hood to reach her door, Noelle used the moment to unsnap her seat belt and collect her handbag. Once he opened the door and reached for her hand, she wasn't at all sure she was ready to feel his warm fingers wrapping around hers. But she had no choice but to accept his help.

Years. That was how long it had been since any man

had made her so aware of every little thing about him. The touch of his warm fingers against hers, the subtle male scent drifting to her nostrils, the strength of his body as she stood close to his side. This man was shoving her senses in all sorts of intimate directions.

The erotic observations left her slightly embarrassed, and as soon as he'd safely helped her to the ground, she eased her hand from his and stepped to one side.

Behind them on the porch, a dog suddenly barked, and a female voice followed.

"Evan! What a surprise! Why didn't you tell us you were coming?"

Noelle turned to see a petite woman dressed in red slacks and a white sweater hurrying toward them. Salt-and-pepper hair was cropped close to her head in a pixie style, and silver earrings swung from her ears. The broad smile on her face was totally genuine, and Noelle felt some of the anxiousness inside her drain away.

Evan shut the truck door, then turned and opened his arms wide to receive his grandmother's fierce hug. As Noelle watched him place a kiss on her cheek, she felt a foolish ball of emotions lodge in her throat.

"I wanted to surprise you, Grandmother," Evan told her.

Laughing with delight, she grabbed him by the arms and pretended to give him a shake. "And what if we'd been gone somewhere? You would've made the drive for nothing."

Chuckling, Evan glanced over at Noelle and winked. "Not hardly. I know where you stash all the food."

With his arm around her waist, he turned his grandmother so that she was facing Noelle. "Grandmother, I want you to meet Noelle Barnes. She's the young lady who found me in the gulch—the one I told you about. She saved my life."

Lady. It had been a long, long time since Noelle had thought of herself as a lady. The fact that Evan perceived her in that way more than surprised her. It left her feeling soft and feminine and almost pretty. Yet it was his last remark that really moved her. Did he honestly think she'd saved his life? Yesterday, he'd said as much to Jessi, but she'd thought he was mostly teasing. She couldn't imagine him giving her that much credit, but apparently he'd already told his grandparents about her and the incident in the gulch.

Evan's grandmother reached for both of Noelle's hands and squeezed them tightly. "Well, it's a real pleasure to meet you, Noelle. My name is Alice."

"Reeves," Evan added for her.

"Bah!" Alice hooted. "Who cares about last names around here? You two come on in the house. Tuck is in the kitchen. We've got an assembly line going."

As the three of them headed toward the house, Evan let out a good-natured groan. "That means she's probably going to put us to work, Noelle."

"You, maybe. Not Noelle. She's a guest, and we don't put guests to work on their first visit."

"We're more interested in eating than working," Evan told her. "Got anything good for lunch?"

"You're lucky," Alice said with a chuckle. "Tuck just happened to want chicken and dumplings today. Otherwise you'd be eating a cheese sandwich."

"Nothing wrong with a cheese sandwich. Especially when you make them, Grandmother. Yours are the best I've ever eaten."

Alice directed a knowing smile at Noelle. "See what a charmer he is? The worst one of the Calhoun bunch."

Evan laughed. "Oh, Grandmother, I couldn't begin to compete with Rafe for that honor, and you know it. Don't give Noelle the wrong ideas about me."

The wrong ideas? Ever since she'd walked up on him that day in the gulch and he'd opened those sexy green eyes, she'd been having wicked thoughts about the man. To hear Alice Reeves describe her grandson as a charmer was hardly any surprise to Noelle. He'd been steadily charming her from the very start. And like a fool, she'd been falling for it.

But today was only one day in her life, she assured herself. After today, she seriously doubted she would ever see the man again. He wasn't interested in her romantically. And even if he was, he'd be the last man on earth she'd let herself fall in love with.

Chapter Five

The plank floor of the porch was only one step off the ground and ran half the length of the Reeves' house. As the three of them walked the length of it to the door, Noelle noticed four white wooden rockers were spaced at intervals. Behind them, next to the wall, was an empty dog bed and a small table with a vase filled with branches of holly and evergreen. The traditional farmhouse was a far different place from the massive ranch house she'd seen when she'd taken Evan home to the Silver Horn.

The brown-and-white shepherd that had been barking earlier was now sitting on his haunches at the door, a grin on his face and a friendly thump to his tail. A yellow tabby nuzzled the dog's side, warily watching the strangers with unblinking green eyes.

"The dog is Rusty and the cat is Ginger," Evan informed Noelle. "And just in case you're worried, neither bite. Go ahead, give them a pat."

"They must like each other," Noelle observed as she reached down and gave both animals an affectionate rub on the head.

"Rusty was just a little pup when we got him, and Ginger was a tiny kitten, so they grew up together. Now they're inseparable," Alice explained. "They sleep, eat, hunt, do everything together. They don't know that one is a dog and the other is a cat. They just know they love each other."

As soon as the older woman opened the door, the animals shot inside. The three of them followed, and once they were all standing inside a small entryway, Noelle was met with the scents of baking cookies, fresh fruit and evergreen.

"Where did Rusty and Ginger go? They must have made a dash for somewhere," Noelle commented.

Alice chuckled. "When the weather is warm, they prefer to be outdoors. But during the winter, they love the kitchen. I think they like being where the action is."

After Evan shut the door, Alice guided them out of the entryway and into a sunny living room. As Noelle looked around, she spotted the source of the evergreen fragrance. A tall blue spruce loaded with decorations stood in front of a pair of paned glass windows. Beneath the branches, several festively wrapped gifts were stacked on the hardwood floor, waiting to be opened on the special day.

The remainder of the area was furnished with a long green couch and matching love seat, two stuffed armchairs in a dark rust color and polished tables covered with crocheted doilies. As they walked through the room, a sense of warmth enveloped Noelle, the same impression of homecoming she'd always gotten whenever she'd walked into her aunt and uncle's home. The feeling was so unexpected and so nice that she was suddenly very glad she'd agreed to accompany Evan today.

After taking their coats and Noelle's handbag and storing them away in a closet, Alice ushered them on to the kitchen. When the three of them entered the room, the first thing Noelle noticed was the tall, dark-haired man with broad shoulders standing at a long work island in the middle of the room. A white apron was tied over his blue chambray shirt, long sleeves rolled back against burly forearms. Upon hearing them enter, he paused in the act of stuffing an orange into a small paper sack. He looked around at the doorway.

Grinning with pleasure, he left the work island and strode over to meet them. "Well, well, darlin', looks like you found us some company," he said to his wife.

"Evan wanted to surprise us, and he surely did. He's brought a lovely young lady with him today," Alice said to her husband. "This is Noelle. She saved our grandson's life, you know. She's a real-life heroine."

Embarrassed by the woman's praise, Noelle shook her head. "That's not the case at all," she said. "All I did was help Evan back onto his horse."

Stepping forward, Tuck reached out to shake her hand. As his big paw closed around her fingers, she forgot that he was a man who'd spent years enforcing the law. Instead, she was simply hoping that he liked her.

"That's not the way Evan explained it all to me," Tuck told her. "He said he was out cold, and you managed to wake him up. Said you found his horse and led Evan out of the gulch when he couldn't see clear enough to find his way out of a paper sack."

"That's right," Evan said, his arm suddenly snaking around the back of Noelle's waist. "Then she took me to the hospital and waited to make sure I was going to live."

Afterward, she'd taken him all the way to the Silver Horn, then deliberately insulted him before leaving him to make it on his own power to the big house, she thought ruefully. Noelle didn't know why he'd been kind enough to spare his grandparents that part of the story. But the fact that he had, coupled with his arm wrapped snugly around her waist, was enough to warm her cheeks.

"We're embarrassing the girl with all this talk," Alice spoke up. She gestured toward a long pine table on the west end of the room. "You two go sit while I take a batch of cookies from the oven. I think the timer is about to go off. Tuck, get them some coffee or something else to drink, won't you, honey?"

"Sure," the older man boomed happily, then slanted a sly grin at Noelle. "A friend just gave me a neat little bottle of apricot brandy for Christmas. Let's have a dose in our coffee. What do you say?"

"I'd say Noelle is going to think you're a naughty old man," Evan teased him.

"It sounds nice and warming," Noelle told him. "I'd like some. But I don't need to sit." She walked over to the work island, with Evan following behind her. "Let me help you two do something. What are all the paper bags for?"

"Oh, I'm filling them with cookies and fruit and homemade toffee," Tuck said. "Alice and I always take the bags to the folks at the local nursing home. Some of them don't get visitors or gifts for Christmas. It's just a little something to let them know they're not forgotten."

"How thoughtful," Noelle murmured.

"While I get the coffee, try the toffee," he urged her. "Alice makes the best. You and Evan can help with the bags after we take our break."

The retired sheriff went over to a long row of white cabinets and began to pull down cups. Evan piled a few pieces of toffee on a plate and motioned for Noelle to join him at the table.

"Isn't that toffee going to ruin your appetite for lunch?" she asked him.

He held out a chair for her. As she eased onto the seat, she noticed the dog and cat were curled together on a pet bed on the floor near a glass patio door. Clearly, the Reeves opened their home to more than friends and family, and Noelle couldn't help but be endeared by the sight of the happy animals.

Laughing, he took a seat to her left, then scooted his chair closer to hers. "This is just an appetizer. Try it."

He held up the piece of toffee, leaving her little option but to lean forward and take a bite without touching her lips to his fingers. Being fed by a handsome man was hardly an everyday occurrence for Noelle, and though she tried to pretend it was nothing, the whole thing felt incredibly intimate to her.

He eagerly watched her crunch the buttery treat. "Good, huh?"

"I'd be in serious trouble if I stayed around here for very long," she replied. "Alice should be running a sweetshop in town."

Evan grinned. "Did you hear that, Grandmother? Noelle says you should open a sweetshop in town."

"Everybody tells her that," Tuck spoke up as he carried a tray filled with red coffee cups over to the table. "But she doesn't have time for that. She's got to stick around here and take care of me."

"Ha," Evan joked. "You mean stick around here and spoil you rotten."

Across the room, Alice placed the cookie sheet on a cooling rack, then joined them at the table. "Once the girls married and moved away, the idea of putting in a bakery did cross my mind," she told Noelle. "But it didn't take me long to decide that getting up at three in the morning would be a bit too early for me."

"I don't think I could handle that, either," Noelle admitted. "Five is early enough for me."

Taking a seat next to her husband, the older woman glanced her way. "You have to be at your job at an early hour?"

"Noelle has a ranch with a nice little herd of cattle. She runs it by herself," Evan said before she had a chance to answer.

"Well, now, that would be a tough job for a big strong man. I'm impressed that you can do it," Tuck told her.

"So am I," Alice added. "Cows terrify me. I'm always afraid they're going to charge at me. And horses are even scarier."

Evan gave his grandmother a playful look. "That's because you never could stay on one. You flop around in the saddle like a rag doll."

Alice rolled her eyes. "I never said I was a bronco buster."

Laughing, Tuck leaned over and gave his wife a peck on the cheek. "No, but if you were, you'd be the prettiest one in Storey County."

Evan chuckled. "I'll bet she'd be the *only* granny bronco buster in Storey County."

Still grinning, Tuck passed the cups of coffee laced with brandy around the table. "Let's make a toast," he suggested.

"Yes, let's," Alice agreed. "This is a special occasion, to have Evan and Noelle surprise us with a visit."

After everyone picked up the cups, Tuck looked at Noelle and smiled. "To you, Noelle, for rescuing our grandson. May you have a blessed Christmas this year and every year."

"Hear, hear," Evan agreed.

Stunned by the simple tribute, Noelle glanced at Evan, who must have read the dismay on her face.

"You can't change Granddad's toast. So don't try," he told her.

"I'm not used to this kind of attention," she murmured. "I don't know what to say. Except thank you all."

"That's enough," Tuck assured her.

The four of them brought their cups together. As Noelle sipped the hot brew, she hoped the splash of brandy would burn away the lump in her throat. She wasn't used to getting this emotional over anything. In fact, she couldn't remember the last time anyone or anything had touched her this much.

For the next few minutes, the four of them munched on the toffee and sipped the coffee while Tuck and Alice related all the local events and gossip that had been going on in the Virginia City area. But then Tuck turned the conversation to Evan's job.

"So tell me, has Sheriff Wainwright been keeping everyone in the office in line?" he asked his grandson.

Before Evan could answer, Alice rose to her feet and reached for Noelle's arm. "Come on, honey," she invited her. "Wyatt Earp here just has to talk law and order for a while or it would kill him. Let me show you what else I've been baking."

Relieved that she didn't have to endure the shoptalk between the two men, Noelle left the table and followed Alice over to the counter, where she'd been filling round tins with cookies and candy.

"I've been making the cookies and the candy all this past week. The rest is out on the back porch. Come on and I'll show you."

At the opposite end of the room, Alice opened a door that led to a long screened-in porch. The space was filled with lawn furniture, an outdoor grill and a wide metal cabinet with double doors.

"I ran out of room in the refrigerator, so I put everything out here to stay nice and cool." Alice opened the cabinet doors. The shelves were filled with baked goods covered in clear cellophane wrap.

"Oh, my! Surely you and Tuck aren't planning to eat all this!" Noelle exclaimed.

Alice chuckled. "Tuck would like to try, but I make him watch his weight—for health reasons, you understand. But I'll keep a few pieces to serve family and friends during Christmas. The rest we'll give out for gifts. There's banana and pumpkin bread. Fruitcake, not the cardboard-tasting kind but the delicious-tasting kind. And then there are fig rolls and prune and apple cakes."

"I can't imagine all the work and expense you've gone to," Noelle told her.

"I enjoy doing it. And giving something personal means more at Christmas, I think." She collected two loaves off the shelf and handed them to Noelle. "Here's a banana bread for you and a pumpkin for Evan. It's his favorite."

"Thank you very much, Alice. I'll enjoy every bite of this."

"Do you do much cooking?" Alice asked as the two of them reentered the kitchen.

"Some. Whenever I have the extra time. I'm not all that good at it, but I try."

Noelle followed Alice over to the counter and placed the two loaves of sweet bread in an out-of-the-way spot.

"What about your mother?" Alice asked as she removed cookies from the cooled metal sheet. "Is she doing a lot of baking for Christmas?"

Noelle had to bite her tongue to keep from letting out

a harsh laugh. The idea of Maxine Barnes wearing an apron over her designer clothing and getting flour on her hands was hilarious, yet at the same time very sad.

"My mother doesn't cook," Noelle said frankly. "I'm not even sure she knows how."

Instead of appearing shocked, Alice merely smiled. "Not everyone is born to like cooking. I just happen to love it. So do your parents live around Carson City?"

Noelle realized Alice wasn't being nosy. She was simply asking normal questions and making polite conversation. She had no way of knowing that Noelle had been estranged from her parents for several years now. Still, it was awkward to explain that sort of thing to a family-oriented woman like Alice.

"No. They live in Phoenix. That is, when they're not traveling. Actually, I don't have much contact with them. We…uh…don't see eye to eye on most things."

Alice's expression turned to one of concern. "Oh. I'm sorry. So you won't be spending Christmas with them?"

"No. My parents are usually out of the country during the holidays, anyway. And since my grandparents are scattered on both coasts, it's too difficult for me to leave the ranch and travel for long distances. So I'll be staying home alone at Christmas."

"I can't imagine Evan allowing that to happen," Alice said with a gentle smile.

From the remark, Noelle could see that Alice was making a romantic connection between Evan and her. Which was only natural. He'd brought her here to his grandparents' home as though she was special. Alice didn't know that he'd merely offered her the outing today as payback for helping him out of the gulch. And Noelle didn't have the heart to tell her.

Smiling faintly, Noelle said, "I'm sure Evan will be very busy during the holidays."

Alice let out a regretful sigh. "Unfortunately, Evan is always busy. When Tuck was still in office, I used to wish crime would stop for at least a week and give him a break. He'd shake his head and remind me that crime never stops. It's a sobering reality."

Suddenly Noelle was seeing the other side of a lawman's life through this woman's eyes and that was a sobering fact to her.

"Alice, did you worry about Tuck's safety back when he was sheriff? That someone might hurt him, shoot him?"

Smiling more to herself than Noelle, Alice pushed a decorative tin down the countertop. "If you don't mind, you can fill that for me. Half cookies and half candy. As for worrying about Tuck, I tried not to, but it was impossible. The badge on his chest made him a target. Still does, even though he's retired. Down through the years, he made enemies of quite a few criminals. You never know when one might return to get revenge. But when you choose to serve the people, you take that risk. I don't allow myself to dwell on that part of our lives, though. Life is too short to live it in fear."

As Noelle methodically placed decorated sugar cookies into the metal container, she wondered whether that was what she'd been doing. Living her life in fear. Afraid to love. Afraid to face the reality of what really happened to her brother. And what if, by some wild chance, something special did develop between her and Evan? Would she constantly worry that he'd be injured or killed on the job?

Not wanting to ruin her day by contemplating such

somber questions, Noelle looked at the other woman. "You're brave, Alice."

Pushing another tin down the counter, Alice gave Noelle a pointed smile. "One of these days, you'll realize just how brave you are, too."

For the next hour, Noelle helped Alice finish packing the cookie tins while Evan and Tuck completed the gift bags. Afterward, for lunch the four of them ate bowls of chicken and dumplings accompanied by corn-bread muffins.

As they sat around the kitchen table, enjoying the good food, the Reeves related stories of when Evan and his brothers were small boys and came to visit their grandparents.

"Evan and Clancy rarely ever broke a rule," Tuck told Noelle, "and the few times they did, they were very apologetic. But Rafe and Finn were another matter. Those two were wild little rascals. And Bowie did his best to keep up with them."

Evan chuckled. "Now Bowie has more discipline than any of us, thanks to the marine corps."

Tuck said, "I had a long visit with him at Clancy and Olivia's wedding reception. He says he'll be coming home to stay in the next few months. I asked him if he was going to help his brothers work the ranch, but he danced around the question."

"I don't think young Bowie has figured out what he wants to do for the rest of his life," Alice said thoughtfully. "For years now, he's had someone telling him what to do. It'll be a big change for him to be his own boss."

Tuck glanced across the table at Noelle. "We've been going on and on about Evan's brothers and sister. We need to hear about you for a while. Do you have any siblings?"

Noelle fought hard not to let everything inside her go cold. Even before she'd set out on this journey with Evan today, she'd expected to be asked the question. It was only natural. Tuck Reeves had no way of knowing that Andy had senselessly lost his life because of a trigger-happy policeman.

Drawing in a deep, bracing breath, she answered, "I had a younger brother. But he died a few years ago."

"Oh, how sad," Alice murmured. "We're so sorry."

Noelle could feel Evan, sitting just to her left, studying her thoughtfully. What would he think, she wondered, if she explained how Andy had died? Would he sympathize and understand her aversion to badges and guns? Or would he be offended?

Oh, God, none of it mattered, she thought. Evan's feelings couldn't be any of her concern. Despite how much she was beginning to enjoy his company, he was still an officer of the law. And though he was a detective, he still went after criminals just like any officer on the street—perhaps with even more determination. Like Tuck, he'd made himself a target.

But none of that really mattered, either, she argued with herself. Evan had no serious intentions toward her. And she had none toward him.

"I know how tough that is," Evan said after a moment. "We had a sister who died when she was two years old. I was only in second grade at the time, but it hit me hard. Rafe was the one who took her death the hardest, though. He was three years old when she was born, and they were growing up together. To this day, he still chokes up when he talks about Darci."

Evan had not only lost his mother, he'd lost a sister,

too. The revelation jolted Noelle. She would've never guessed that he'd gone through such tragedy. He seemed too strong and sturdy, too happy to have endured such sorrow.

"Well, the two of them were like Rusty and Ginger," Alice explained. "Brother and sister were inseparable."

Tuck reached over and patted his wife's hand as though he wanted to soften the sad memory of their granddaughter's death. "Now Rafe has a little girl of his own to coddle and spoil. Thank God he's been blessed with her."

Alice suddenly turned an impish smile on Evan. "We're hoping that someday Evan will have a few kids."

Tuck looked over and winked at Noelle. "Yeah, Evan's getting a little long in the tooth. He's going to be too old to be a daddy if he keeps waiting around to find the right woman."

Evan grimaced. "You two needn't be worried about me. You'll get plenty of great-grandkids to spoil without me contributing to the family tree."

Even though on the surface he was kidding, Noelle could hear a thread of resentment in his voice. Apparently he didn't want anyone, even his beloved grandparents, pushing him toward love and marriage and children. So what did that mean? Had someone broken his heart before, or did he simply enjoy being a bachelor too much to give up his freedom?

Tuck's low chuckles lightened the moment. Noelle looked across the table to see he was eyeing her and Evan as though they were already a couple. The notion bothered Noelle, mainly because she'd already allowed her daydreams to go in that same foolish direction.

"We better stop nagging our grandson, Alice. He knows what's best for him."

"You've got that right, Granddad." Evan rose to his feet abruptly and reached for the back of Noelle's chair. "Now if you two will excuse us, I'd like to show Noelle around outside before we have to leave."

Later that afternoon, Evan drove west to give Noelle a chance to view the beautiful landscape at Washoe Lake before finishing the long drive back to her house.

When he finally stopped the truck in front of her house, it was growing dark. He cut the engine and unsnapped his seat belt, prompting her to speak.

"There's no need for you to get out," she assured him. "I can make it to the door on my own."

A subtle grin slanted his lips. "Trying to get rid of me?"

For the past thirty minutes, she'd been steeling herself to the reality that this special day had to end. She'd been telling herself that she needed to give this man a final goodbye and make a rock-hard promise to herself never to see him again. That would be the smart thing to do. But now he was hinting that he wanted their time together to continue. How could she possibly tell him to leave when her heart was thumping hard, begging her to invite him to stay?

"Not exactly." Trying to ignore the tempting sight of his rugged face, she released her seat belt and reached behind her for the coat she'd placed on the backseat. "But it's getting late, and I have chores to do."

"That's why I'm not going to leave just yet. It's my fault that I kept you out after dark. The least I can do is help you with the chores."

She squared around in the seat so that she was facing him. "Is this something you do with all your dates? Offer to help them with their chores?" Before he could answer, she shook her head. "Sorry. I wasn't thinking. I'm not your date. So forget my question."

A half-amused look came over his face. "If you're not my date, what are you?"

Before she'd met Evan, a blush rarely ever touched Noelle's cheeks. But something about this man seemed to be turning her whole face into a perpetual heat lamp.

"I'm not sure. An acquaintance, maybe. I haven't exactly thought about it," she lied.

Before she could guess his intentions, he leaned across the console and brought his face close to hers. "Maybe I ought to give you a little clue."

He was so near, she could see the amber flecks in his green eyes, the pores in his tanned skin and the faintly jagged outline of his hard lips. And as her eyes settled on the last feature, her heart began to thump out of control.

"What are you talking about?" she whispered.

His face inched closer, and for the life of her, she couldn't seem to draw back or turn her head to avoid his. All day long, she'd thought about being close to him, kissing him. She'd never expected to be given that chance, and now it felt as though she was caught in a dream. One where she couldn't breathe or move, even though her mind was screaming at her to make a quick escape.

His lips hovering over hers, he murmured, "I think I need to show you that you're more than an acquaintance to me, Noelle."

Confusion stunned her brain, and then suddenly she couldn't think at all as he closed the last fraction of space between their lips.

The movement of his hard mouth over hers was both shocking and delicious. The mixture was enough to make her fingers unwittingly close over the tops of his shoulders and a low groan to sound in her throat.

And as her mind began to digest the reality that she was kissing a lawman, her heart argued that Evan Calhoun was simply a man. A man who was filling her with excitement and chasing away the lonely shadows she'd carried around for so long.

Chapter Six

Evan could've gone on kissing Noelle for hours, but the need for oxygen eventually forced him to lift his head from hers and drag in several ragged breaths. It was then he noticed that her fingers were still clinging to his shoulders and her eyes remained shut.

Clearly, she'd been as shaken by what had just occurred between them as he'd been. And for the first time in his life, he didn't know what to say or how to react. What had started out as a simple kiss had turned into something he'd never experienced before.

"I—uh, I didn't plan on that happening," he finally murmured.

Her eyes slowly opened, and she dropped her hands away from him. The loss of contact made Evan want to pull her into his arms and repeat the heart-stopping kiss all over again.

"Neither did I," she said softly.

"I'm sorry if I upset you."

She looked away from him, and her shoulders moved up and down as she drew in a deep breath.

"You didn't upset me. It was just a kiss."

It hadn't been just a kiss to him. It had been an earthquake. But he couldn't admit that to this woman. He didn't even like admitting it to himself.

Before he could think of a reply, she turned back to

him. "So does this mean you were thinking of me as a date?"

He had to laugh. The sound put a faint smile on her face.

"Well, I normally don't kiss on first dates," she said. "But since I haven't had one in years, I guess I can forgive myself." She reached for the door latch. "I can hear the cows bawling. I'd better get to my chores."

Her comment about dating filled Evan with questions, but he kept them to himself. Now wasn't the time to be asking her personal questions. Besides, her private life wasn't his concern. Even though that kiss had made him feel as though it was.

"Come on," he said. "I'll show you that I know a little about taking care of livestock."

A little more than a half hour later, Evan was sitting at Noelle's kitchen table, eating the last few bites of a ham sandwich and drinking a cup of coffee. The fact that she'd invited him in for a light evening meal surprised him. After he'd helped her deal with the chores at the barn, he'd expected her to give him a firm goodnight. But she'd seemed grateful for his help and even his company.

Now Evan couldn't keep his eyes off her or his mind from reliving her kiss over and over. He'd never tasted lips so sweet and soft and giving. The fragrance of her hair and skin had filled his nostrils like the heady scent of a flower garden. As her lips eagerly met his searching lips, his senses had reeled like a helter-skelter whirlwind dancing over the desert floor.

"Would you like a piece of the banana bread that your grandmother sent home with me?" She rose from the table and carried her plate over to the sink.

"No, thanks. I've already eaten enough for two people today."

She brought the coffee carafe back to the table and topped off both their cups. Evan couldn't ignore the subtle swing of her hips as she returned the glass pot to the coffee machine. The thought of touching those womanly curves, of pressing his body next to them, was enough to make his heart beat fast and a heat burn low in his belly.

After taking to her seat again, she picked up her cup but didn't immediately take a sip. Instead, her thoughtful gaze wandered over him. "Would you mind if I asked you something personal?"

Surprisingly, it was the intensity of her gaze rather than her question that made him want to squirm in his chair. Something about the way she looked at him was daring and sexy, and he found it impossible to tear his eyes away from hers.

He said, "I'd have to hear the question first."

Shrugging, her gaze dropped to the scarred tabletop. "Well, it's not really my business. But today, when your grandparents were talking about you marrying and having kids, I got the impression that you were totally against the idea. Am I right?"

"Pretty much," he said bluntly.

Glancing up at him, she asked, "And why is that? Have you been married before?"

He tried not to let bitter memories show on his face. "No. I was engaged once—about four years ago. But it didn't work out."

She returned her cup to the tabletop. "Oh. You got cold feet? Or did she?"

Shaking his head, he made an attempt to smile, but

in truth there was nothing about his failed relationship with Bianca to smile about.

"The problem wasn't cold feet. It was all about having my eyes opened. And thankfully, that happened before any marriage ceremony took place." Grimacing, he pushed aside his empty plate and picked up his coffee cup. "You see, I thought Bianca was just right for me. When we first started dating, she was sweet and understanding. She seemed to really care about me. I even believed she was proud of my profession and understood how much it meant to me. But it turned out that she was hiding the real her. That is, until our wedding date grew closer and she started making demands."

"What sort of demands?"

"That I quit the sheriff's office and return to working for the Silver Horn."

Her dark brown eyes continued to search his face, and Evan could only wonder what she was thinking. That he wasn't man enough to hold a woman? The notion bothered him more than it should have.

"And why was that?" she asked softly. "Because she worried for your safety?"

With a short, caustic laugh, Evan rose, carried his empty plate over to the sink and placed it on top of hers.

"She often said she was worried about my safety, and maybe it did worry her," he answered. "But I don't think the danger associated with my job was the main reason our relationship ended. She harped more about the modest income I made. She knew that if I worked on the Silver Horn, my annual salary from the ranch's profits would be far better than that of a deputy sheriff. In the end, it became clear to me and everyone that she was all about getting a piece of the Calhoun wealth."

A long pause ensued. Then Noelle asked, "So you don't receive any annuities from the ranch?"

Shaking his head, he turned away from the cabinet. "No. Without doing my part, it wouldn't be right for me to accept them. I do get a yearly slice of mineral royalties that my mom willed to us boys. But I don't spend it. I tuck all that away for a rainy day."

She remained silent until Evan returned to the table and eased back into his seat. By then she was looking at him with an entirely different expression. One that drew him like a beckoning light in a dark and dangerous cave.

"I guess now when you meet a woman, you're always wondering whether she's after your money or she's genuinely interested in you."

He let out a long breath. "I'm surprised to hear you say that. I didn't think you'd understand. I mean, you've made your opinion about lawmen pretty clear. I figured you'd think Bianca had a good argument for me to quit the office."

Frowning, she rose to her feet and walked over to the stack of dirty dishes. Evan wondered what she was thinking as she began to fill the sink with water. That he was selfish? That he cared only about himself and his career? Before now, that wouldn't have bothered him. It certainly hadn't bothered him when Bianca had flung those accusations at him. But Noelle was different. She was independent and strong and sensible. And more than anything, he wanted her to think he was a fair, admirable man.

"You have me figured all wrong, Evan."

Her quiet reply had him joining her at the counter. "About what?"

She plunged her hands into the dishwater and swiped

one of the plates. "Whatever my feelings about law officers are, I think this Bianca was selfish for asking you to give up a career that you love—that you've wanted from a very young age. That's not what love and marriage are about."

Stunned by her answer, he shook his head in disbelief. "You sound like you're talking from experience."

She cast him a thoughtful glance, then abruptly pulled her hands from the sink and dried them on a dish towel.

"Come with me," she said. "I need to show you something."

Not knowing what to expect, Evan followed her out of the kitchen and into the small living area, where she motioned for him to take a seat.

"Make yourself comfortable," she told him. "I'll be right back."

She left the room and he'd barely had time to get settled on the couch when she returned carrying a fabric-covered notebook.

To his surprise, she didn't hand the book to him. Instead, she sat down close by his side and balanced it on her knees. By then, Evan didn't really care what was on the pages of the padded notebook. All he could think about was the warmth of her body radiating into his, the scent of her skin and hair and the softness of her feminine curves.

"I haven't looked at this thing for a long time," she told him. "In fact, it's crossed my mind more than once to throw it away. But I keep it as a learning tool. So I won't forget and make the same mistake again."

For a moment, curiosity pushed his erotic thoughts aside. "Mistake?" he asked. "What's inside this thing, anyway?"

"My wedding photos."

She could have said anything and it wouldn't have shocked him more. "Wedding?" he repeated blankly. "You've been married before?"

Her lips pressed in a grim line, she nodded. "That's right. When I still lived in Phoenix. We were married a little less than a year."

"Less than a year? Damn," he murmured. "That was short."

Her nostrils flared with disdain. "If I'd known his true colors beforehand, there wouldn't have been a marriage at all."

Stunned, he tried to imagine her as some other man's wife. Try as he might, he couldn't envision her being so close to anyone but him. And that notion in itself was enough to leave him speechless and wondering what in hell could be coming over him.

She opened the cover of the photo album, and Evan was given another shock. It was evident that the wedding had been professionally photographed, costing someone a fortune. But it was Noelle's image that grabbed his attention. She looked nothing like the woman sitting next to him.

Instead, her features were hidden behind a mask of perfect makeup, her long brown hair coiffed into an elaborate pile of curls and adorned with a glittering tiara. The white lace dress she wore swept the floor with a full skirt. A jeweled choker created a garland of gems around her lovely neck. Admittedly, Evan didn't know that much about women's fashion or the cost, but he knew enough to spot luxury when he saw it. And it all made him wonder if he was sitting next to a complete stranger.

"This is you?" He couldn't hide the disbelief in his voice. "When was this?"

"That's me. About five years ago. I've changed since then. In more ways than one."

"I'll say," he murmured, dazed.

She chuckled, but it was a cynical sound, mocking instead of amused.

"You see, Evan, I know all about having money. What it's like to have anything and everything it can buy. I also know all the things it can't buy."

She tapped her forefinger against the face of the groom. Though Evan didn't want to, he took a closer look at the blond man dressed in a dark tuxedo.

"That was Phillip. We met when he came to work for my father. At that time, I worked in the family business, too, as a secretary for one of the building contractors. Phillip had been hired as more of an assistant, someone to take care of the boring details of the business. He was the cheery, charming sort, and we hit it off almost immediately. When he asked me to marry him, I believed he truly loved me. That he wanted us to have children and a real marriage. And for ten months he pretended to be a loving husband."

"Pretended?"

"That's what I said. I discovered quite by accident that he'd married me to work his way up the ladder in my father's company. He never loved me at all."

"I probably have no right to ask, but how did you find out?"

Shaking her head, she let out a weary sigh. "Believe me, Evan, it wasn't like I had a private investigator digging up ugly secrets and reporting them back to me. I didn't have a clue that my husband was hiding anything from me. One evening I came in from a trip to the

grocery store. When I walked by the den, I could hear
Phillip talking with Reggie, one of his work friends.
I started to enter the room and say hello when Phillip
chuckled in a smug way. Something about the sound
made me pause outside the door and listen."

"I'm sure you've heard the old saying about eavesdropping," Evan commented. "You usually hear something you're not going to like."

Rising from the couch, she snapped the photo album
shut, then tossed it onto the cushion next to Evan. A
part of him wanted to pick it up and flip through the
pages. Seeing glimpses of her past life would tell him
a great deal about the woman standing before him now.
But then, like eavesdropping, he might see things about
her that he didn't like. And he didn't want that to happen. Spending time with her was becoming special to
him. He wanted it to stay special.

She walked across the small room and began to
straighten a stack of mail lying on the end of a rolltop
desk. "That's an understatement," she said sourly. "He
told Reggie that he would've never married a woman
so coarse and plain if it hadn't been for my old man's
money."

Her voice was cool and level, as though she was talking about something as mundane as carrying out the
garbage. But Evan had learned to read people's voices
even more than their facial expressions. He sensed she
was doing her best to cover up years of pain. The idea
bothered him.

"I know this is going to sound stupid," he said after
a moment, "but what did you do? Hell, I've encountered
women who would've gone after a man like Phillip with
a gun or knife and never blinked an eye."

She looked around at him and he noticed her lips had taken on a wry slant.

"I probably should have felt violent, but I was actually more frozen than anything. I kept standing there listening and trying to figure out how I'd married such a monster. And then, just when I thought it might be best to walk in and let my presence be known, he began to talk about my dad and the company. So I stood there hidden out of sight behind the doorjamb, like a voyeur in my own home."

Sensing that she'd yet to get to the crux of the matter, he asked, "What kind of company does your dad own?"

Returning to the couch, she eased back down beside him. "Dad is a land developer. He takes a piece of property and turns it into a strip mall or something that will eventually make money. You see, making money is what Dad is all about. And believe me, Evan, over the years he's made lots of it."

Suddenly a few pieces of the puzzle were fitting together. Like all the wealth Evan could see in the wedding photos. But for the most part, her revelation simply filled him with more questions. He gestured to the room around them.

"I don't understand, Noelle. You're not living in wealth."

Her short burst of laughter was nothing but harsh as she picked up the photo album. "Let me show you just one more picture. That's all it will take to explain the sort of life I used to lead."

She opened the album and rested the right half on his knee. Evan reluctantly leaned forward to look at the glossy image.

"That was taken at the wedding reception. As you can see, hundreds of people were there." She pointed to a couple, somewhere in their late forties, standing side by side, drinking from long-stemmed glasses. "Here are my parents. They insisted that everything for their daughter's wedding be done in grand style."

The sarcasm in her voice had him looking at her with confusion. "There are plenty of young women who dream of having this kind of wedding, Noelle. You didn't like it?"

"I hated it. But I didn't have a say in the matter. I never had much of a say about anything. Back then, I was more of a submissive person. I wanted them to be proud of me, and more than anything, I wanted their love. So I'd go along and let them run my life. That's one of the reasons I ended up marrying Phillip in the first place. Dad kept insisting that he was a great catch and I could do no better. At the time, I didn't have a clue that my father had been making dishonest business deals for years and that he'd promised to bring Phillip in on the profits as an incentive to marry me."

Not bothering to ask permission, Evan closed the album and placed it on the end table sitting next to him. "So that's what you heard the day outside the den?"

Nodding, she dropped her gaze away from him. "After I promptly told Phillip I was divorcing him, I confronted my parents. They laughed at my outrage and insinuated that I was ungrateful and even a little weird for having morals. The next day, I had every penny in my bank account transferred to my dad's business account. I wanted nothing to do with his dirty deals. And nothing more to do with my parents."

Evan squared around on the cushion so he was facing her. "I recall you saying that your aunt and uncle willed you this place. When did that happen?"

Her brown eyes were suddenly shadowed with sorrow and Evan very much wanted to reach over and draw her into his arms. He wanted to tell her that she was one of the bravest women he'd ever met. He wanted to assure her that she wasn't alone. But she wouldn't understand such a reaction from him. How could she? Even he didn't understand the feelings she was stirring inside him.

"The traffic accident that took Aunt Geneva and Uncle Rob had occurred only about three weeks before the blowup with my husband and parents. At that time, I was unaware they'd willed me this land. Later, I was in the process of finding a place to move when I got a call from their lawyer about this land in Nevada. He thought I wouldn't be interested and was offering to find a Realtor to put it on the market. You see, my aunt and uncle left a stipulation in the will that I had to live on the land and work it. Otherwise, it would be sold and the money given to charity. Even before everything that happened with Phillip and my parents, they understood I wasn't living the kind of life I needed and wanted. Getting this ranch was—well, it was like a gift straight from heaven."

"So you knew immediately that you wanted to come here?"

Nodding, she said, "I had no idea what it looked like, but I didn't care. Along with the land, Geneva and Rob left me a small amount of money—enough to make the move and buy a few cattle. So here I am."

Yes, here she was, Evan thought. Eking out a meager living after being raised in a life of luxury. It was incredible, and yet her whole journey to get to this patch of desert land inspired him and drew him even closer to her.

"When you talked about Bianca wanting you to give

up your career, I understood, Evan. My parents argued and insisted that taking care of a bunch of dirty cows wouldn't make me happy. They vowed I would want to come back to Phoenix someday, whenever I got tired and broke and hungry. But I promise you, that day will never come."

The conviction in her voice had him searching her face. "And what about Phillip? Does he expect you to come back to him someday?"

A grimace marred her lovely features. "At first, he didn't want to let me go. And I'm not sure why. He never loved me, and he certainly didn't respect me. I suppose he thought that if he hung on to me, he could hang on to his job with Dad. But that would've never happened. Dad was furious with him for shooting his mouth off so recklessly and fired him. And I was leaving for Nevada for good. I suppose, in the end, Phillip got what he deserved."

Evan couldn't stop himself from reaching over and clasping her hand in his. "I'm glad you shared this with me, Noelle. What I went through with Bianca was nothing compared with your ordeal."

Rather than look at him, she gazed at their coupled hands. "Don't feel bad for me, Evan. I'm better off for it. I'm smarter. Stronger. Happier."

His thumb spread across the back of her hand and gently rubbed the soft skin. "Since you moved here, you've not wanted to get back into dating? You haven't thought about marrying again?"

Her gaze lifted to his, and Evan could see that his question had surprised her.

"No. Why would I want to?"

Why indeed? he thought. He got the same questions about dating and marriage from his family, and he resented their prying into his private feelings. No one seemed to understand that Bianca had ruined his trust in women and himself.

"Yeah," he said. "Well, I think it's different for a woman. You need things in your life that a man can do without."

There was something soft and seeking about her gaze as it gently roamed his face. He felt desire stir deep within him.

"You mean like babies and love?" she asked.

Evan felt ridiculous. What was he doing having such a conversation with this woman? These weren't topics he discussed with anyone, so why was he doing it now?

Because something about her makes you think of family and home and all the soft things a man couldn't make for himself. Because for the first time in a long time, you've met a woman who doesn't bore you. One who stirs every masculine cell in you.

The bold challenge in her eyes, coupled with the voice going off in his head, was enough to send a rush of heat to his face.

"Well, it's natural for a woman to want those things, isn't it?" he countered.

A faint smile tilted the corners of her lips. "I thought it was natural for a man to want those things, too."

"You're right. They do. Two of my brothers wanted love and babies enough to get married. But I—I'm not sure those things are for me."

Sighing, she eased away from him and rose to her feet. "I'm not sure those things are for me, either," she said, then smiled at him. "I'd better go finish the dishes before the water goes cold."

She could be lounging around in a mansion, he thought, with a cook, plenty of maids and any luxury she wanted. Instead, she was taking care of livestock and living in an old, tiny stucco with only the barest necessities.

Leaving the couch, he placed a hand on her arm to detain her. Her reaction was to arch a questioning brow at him.

"Before you do that, I—" He made the mistake of letting his gaze settle on her lips, and his thoughts suddenly went haywire. One kiss, he thought, and that was all it had taken to make him desperate for another.

"You what?" she prompted him.

Feeling like a randy teenager, he mentally shook himself. "I just wanted to say how much I admire your courage. You reached out for what you wanted and didn't let anyone or anything sway you. I'd like to think I was that brave. But I'm not."

"You're giving me too much credit. Besides, you're a law officer. I'm sure you've put yourself in all sorts of dangerous situations before. You have to be brave to do the job you do."

He grimaced. "Yeah, I've faced a few weapon-wielding criminals before. Knife blades, baseball bats. I've even had someone come at me with a hay hook. But that's not the kind of bravery I was talking about. You left a comfortable life, the only kind you'd ever known, to strike out on your own. I haven't been able to do that."

"What do you mean? You've already told me how you went against your family's wishes and became a law officer. You bucked tradition."

"Yeah. But I'm still living on the ranch to appease my grandfather. I'm still driving seventy miles round-trip to work every day in order to keep him and my dad happy. I don't have the courage to move away and disappoint either of them."

"Or the comfortable life you have there," she added with a knowing smile. "But that's where your family is, Evan. Your loved ones. That's where the difference between our situations lies. Back in Phoenix, I didn't have anyone who really loved me. I was a possession, a decoration of sorts for my parents. And little more than a stepping stone for Phillip. When I moved here, I had nothing to lose and everything to gain."

She was making too much sense. And being this close to her was definitely feeling too good. When Evan first started talking, he should've dropped his hold on her arm, but touching her for any reason was a pleasure he couldn't pass up.

"Maybe you're right," he told her. "Anyway, it's getting late, and I have to be at work early in the morning. I'll help you finish those dishes, and then I'd better go."

She let out a short chuckle. "Two plates, two cups and forks? I think I can manage those on my own."

Not wanting to leave, but knowing it was inevitable, he said, "I'll get my jacket and hat from the kitchen."

Dropping his hold on her arm, he went to the other room to fetch the items. When he returned to the living area, Noelle was gone, and so was the photo album he'd placed on the end table.

Apparently she'd wanted to put the images away and out of sight. But the memories—where did she put them? he wondered. Did she still think of her ex-husband and wish that he could have loved her?

Stop thinking about it, Evan. Noelle isn't looking for a man. Especially a lawman. And you aren't looking for a woman. Not on a permanent basis.

The sound of her footsteps pushed the mocking voice

from his mind, and he turned to see her reentering the room. To his surprise, she walked straight over to him and linked her arm through his.

"I'll walk you to the door," she said impishly.

He chuckled in the same way she had when he'd offered to wash the handful of dishes. "It's less than five feet away. I think I can make it."

The smile on her face faded, and Evan felt his heartbeat kick into a faster gear.

"When you gave me that kiss in the truck, you implied that our outing today was a date. So as your date, I should walk with you to the door," she murmured. "Cowgirls are tough, but we do have manners, you know."

Without even realizing how it happened, Evan suddenly found the two of them at the door with his back pressed against the wooden panel and her face tilted invitingly up to his.

"Good night, Evan. Thank you again for today. Your grandparents were such a treat. I'm very glad that you gave me the chance to meet them."

"They enjoyed you, too. And so did I."

Her head bent downward. "Evan, about that kiss… I…"

When her words awkwardly trailed away, he wrapped his thumb and forefinger around her chin and lifted her face up to his. "Noelle, I can't quit thinking about that kiss," he whispered. "And you must be thinking about it, too."

Doubt suddenly shadowed her brown eyes. "Yes. And I've been thinking it was— Well, I just wanted you to know that I don't go around kissing a man that way. I mean, I don't go around kissing any man. And I'm not sure why I—" She broke off abruptly and turned her back to him. "I think I've given you the wrong impression."

Resting his hands gently on her shoulders, he said, "I wasn't exactly resisting. I probably gave you the wrong impression, too. But I don't care. I feel something special with you. And it has nothing to do with you saving my life."

She groaned. "Saving your life," she repeated. "That whole notion is ridiculous."

Gently, he turned her around to him, only to find a torn expression on her face.

"What's ridiculous is how much I want to kiss you again," he murmured.

Her eyes widened and her lips parted, but Evan didn't wait to see if she was going to reply. He was finished with waiting. Instead, he swiftly bent his head and fastened his lips over hers.

This time the console of the truck wasn't separating them, and Evan took advantage by wrapping his arms around her and drawing her tightly against him.

The feel of her soft, womanly curves melting into him and yielding to his searching hands sent Evan's senses into heated overdrive. Before he knew it, his mouth was rocking hungrily over hers, his tongue seeking the warmth beyond her lips.

He wanted this woman. So much so that he forgot where he was. Forgot the long, reckless minutes ticking by. Until she suddenly pulled herself out of his arms. Then reality came sweeping in, jerking him out of the clouds and back to the modest living room.

With her hand against her lips, she stepped away and stared at him for long seconds before she finally turned and raced out of the room.

Evan's first instinct was to run after her and force her

to talk about what had just occurred between them. But as he heard a door slam in another part of the house, he realized that she needed to be alone. They both needed space and time to cool off, and then maybe they could figure out what exactly they meant to each other.

But a few moments later, as Evan climbed into his truck and drove away from Noelle's lonely little house, he realized that neither time nor space would be enough to wipe her from his mind.

Chapter Seven

Three days later, Noelle walked into the Grubstake Café and took a seat at the long bar. Since the Tuesday morning was growing late and lunch-hour traffic hadn't yet arrived, the diner was quiet except for the Christmas music playing on a radio behind the bar. The few customers scattered around the room were more interested in eating than talking.

"Noelle! When did you come in?"

At the sound of Jessi's voice, Noelle looked toward the swinging double doors that separated the kitchen from the dining area. At the moment, the batwing doors were still rocking on their hinges from Jessi shouldering her way through them.

"About five seconds ago," she told the waitress. "I was afraid your shift had already ended."

"Not a chance," Jessi said with a weary smile, then inclined her head toward the tray of food she was carrying in both hands. "I'll be right back."

While she waited for Jessi to return, Noelle pulled off her jacket and draped it over her lap. Since she'd driven into town only to pay the waitress for her bill from the other day, she hadn't taken the time to put on makeup or change out of her work clothes. And though she realized she looked worn and shabby, she wasn't concerned that she might run into Evan. In fact, it would probably be good for him to see her like this. Maybe then he wouldn't get the urge to kiss her again.

Why are you worried about that, Noelle? After running to your bedroom and slamming the door, you've neither seen nor heard from the man. He's clearly decided that you're too crazy for him. And that was all for the best.

The mocking voice in her head was probably right, Noelle thought. But a part of her wasn't yet convinced that she'd seen the last of the deputy sheriff. When he'd kissed her that last time at the door, he'd known all about her baggage. She'd made it clear to him that she'd given her small fortune back to her parents and that she would never be rich again. She'd even confessed to him that she wasn't looking for a man. Yet he'd kissed her anyway, and nothing about the way his lips had moved over hers had felt as if he was disinterested.

"Okay, here I am," Jessi announced as she hurried behind the bar. She stopped in front of Noelle. "What would you like? Coffee? Cinnamon roll?"

"Right now I want to pay you for my bill from the other day. Do you remember the amount?"

The redheaded waitress waved a hand. "Forget it. Consider it my treat."

Noelle opened her handbag and pulled out her wallet. "Thanks, but no way will I let you pay for my absent-mindedness."

While Jessi rolled her eyes with disapproval, Noelle placed a bill large enough to cover the cost on the countertop.

"Why can't you accept things without an argument?" Jessi wanted to know.

"Because I know you're like me. You need every

dime you make. That's why. Now you quit arguing and take the money."

Seeing that Noelle was serious, Jessi stuffed the bill into a pocket of her apron, then rested her elbows on the countertop.

"So, are you ready to tell me about this thing with you and Evan Calhoun? When I first saw you two talking together the other day, you could've knocked me over with a feather."

The warm café held the homey scents of bacon, coffee and apple pie, and Noelle realized that since she'd moved to the Carson City area, it was one of the few places she'd come to feel comfortable in. Probably because it was simple and mostly full of hardworking people like Jessi.

"There's nothing to tell, Jess, other than what Evan said about me finding him in the gulch."

"Well, something sure had you stirred up the other day. You've never left here without paying before!"

Noelle grimaced. "I didn't do it on purpose, Jess."

The waitress let out an annoyed wail. "I never thought you did. I'm just saying—"

"Okay, okay, I'll admit it. Evan did have me stirred. He'd asked me out."

Jessi's blue eyes grew wide. Then, leaning closer, she lowered her voice. "You mean, like out on a date?"

"He considered it one. But I didn't. We went to visit his grandparents up near Virginia City."

"Oh, my! That's even more important than a date! How in the world did this happen? Had you ever met him before that day he had the accident?"

"No. I'd never heard of the Calhoun family or the Silver Horn Ranch. But then, you know my social circle is limited to this café, the feed store and the grocery store. I don't keep up with local news or events."

Jessi sighed as though a Cinderella story was actually unfolding before her very eyes. Noelle refrained from groaning out loud.

"I can't imagine what it must have been like to be with a man like him. He's so—" Jessi's expression turned starry-eyed. "Strong and rugged. And the way he looks in his white shirt and jeans. It's like he's all shoulders and long legs. Sometimes he's wearing a badge on his chest and a pistol on his hip, and that's when he looks like nobody else in the room. But I guess you've already noticed that."

"Apparently, not as much as you," Noelle said wryly.

Jessi let out a sheepish laugh. "Sorry. I guess I did sound a little dreamy, didn't I? But gee, it's just so exciting to hear about you going out with Detective Calhoun. Did you visit the big ranch?"

"No. And before you start getting all these ideas, there was nothing romantic about the day. It was just a simple outing. That's all."

Well, except for those two kisses, that was mostly the truth, Noelle thought.

Shouldering her handbag, she rose to her feet. "I'd better be going. I have a lot to do back at the ranch."

Jessi frowned. "You're not going to have anything to eat? At least stay long enough for coffee."

"Not this morning. I came by just to settle my bill. I'll see you later."

Rounding the bar, Jessi followed Noelle to the door.

"Why don't you drive back into town tonight and watch the Christmas parade? Come by my apartment and we'll go together. It'll be fun."

"Thank you for asking, Jess, but I don't want to burn all that gasoline just to watch a parade."

Jessi scowled at her. "Just a parade! Noelle, how can you be so jaded? It's the Christmas parade!"

Feeling ashamed of herself, Noelle wiped a weary hand over her face. "I'm sorry. I didn't mean it that way. I'm just not in a festive mood."

With her birthday drawing near, she couldn't help thinking how her father had sometimes called her his Christmas baby. But that had been when she was a young child and years before she'd learned the truth about him and Phillip being partners in deception. So much had changed in her life since then. Her brother was gone, and her parents were not much more than a tangle of fond and painful memories. Now she had no close family to acknowledge her birthday or to join her in celebrating Christmas. Evan had implied that this year, the holidays might be different for her. But she couldn't imagine how. She didn't have someone like his grandparents to envelop her in warm love. She didn't have someone like him to kiss her beneath the mistletoe.

Folding her arms, Jessi studied Noelle with disapproval. "You're never in a festive mood. I don't get it, Noelle. You told me that you moved here to the Carson City area so you could be happy. I'm not sure you've ever reached that state of mind."

"Well, thanks for reminding me that I'm a sour bore," Noelle retorted, then opened the door and stepped onto the narrow concrete sidewalk that ran alongside the front of the café.

Ever persistent, Jessi followed. "Okay, run home and pretend that you're not lonely and miserable. That will fix everything."

"I don't want anything *fixed*. I'm happy just as I am.

Now you'd better get back inside before a customer starts hollering for a waitress."

Giving Jessi a wave, she climbed into her truck and drove away from the Grubstake. But once she was completely out of her friend's view, her shoulders slumped and tears burned her eyes.

Run home and pretend that you're not lonely and miserable.

Was Jessi right? Was that what she'd been doing the past four years since she'd come to Nevada? Pretending that her heart was healed and ready to find love and happiness? No. She wasn't fooling anyone, including herself. If she was over the past, then she would've wrapped her arms around Evan and hung on tightly. Instead, she'd run from him and all the passion he was making her feel.

Later that day, Evan was working in his office when his partner walked into the small room. Vincent Parcell, tall with dark hair, took a seat on a corner of Evan's cluttered desk.

Evan asked, "Have a nice lunch?"

"Lunch, hell! Where did you get that idea? I've been working the pharmacy robbery for the past three hours. Why didn't you show up?"

Leaning back in the chair, Evan pointed to the report lying in front of him. "Before I could leave the building, Captain Ridder caught me. He said you could handle the pharmacy case. He wanted me to look at this."

Now thirty-two, Vincent had been working in the investigation arm of the office for two years when Evan had been promoted to detective. Since then, the men had become close friends. Though there wasn't that much difference in their work experience, Evan felt as though Vincent was light-years ahead of him in finding evidence that others missed.

"What is it?" Vincent asked.

"The coroner's report on Watson's body. He's ruled it a homicide."

Vincent rubbed a hand against the day-old stubble covering his jaws. "Not too much of a surprise there. It wasn't like the man had any reason to be on a country road without a vehicle or anything around."

"Right. Well, listen to this," Evan said. "The coroner discovered a needle puncture in his back. Someone injected him with a lethal dose of phenylbutazone."

A thoughtful frown wrinkled Vincent's lean features. "Isn't that the stuff you use on horses for pain?"

"That's right. It's normally called bute by ranchers and the people who deal with horses."

"So that bruised-looking area on the shoulder—the spot we thought was from a blow or a fall—was that where the stuff was injected?"

Evan nodded. "If the drug is administered into muscle, it destroys the tissue."

"Hmm. Don't figure Watson stabbed himself in the back."

"No more than he carried himself to that country back road and then fell over dead in the pasture." To think they'd found the corpse only a couple of miles from Noelle's house sent a cold shiver down Evan's spine. She might not lock her doors whenever she was out of the house, but he was going to make damned sure she locked them at night before she went to bed.

"Watson wasn't a rancher," Vincent reasoned. "He was a truck driver. And from what his family and friends told us, he'd been out of work for several months.

Where could the killer have gotten this drug? Is it only dispensed through a vet?"

"Yeah. It's a controlled substance. But most ranches will have a bottle of it sitting around in case of emergency. It also comes in paste form for oral use, but clearly that doesn't come into play with Watson's death."

Vincent eased off the desk and walked a few steps over to his own desk. As he took a seat in the swivel chair behind it, he said, "Well, now we've got to go through all the man's contacts and try to figure out which one of them could've had access to the drug. Shouldn't be that hard to figure out which ones work around horses or ranching."

Evan shook his head. "Before you start getting tunnel vision, Vince, you might need to know that dogs are sometimes treated with it, too, and in a few cases, even people. Not very often. But the possibility is there."

"Oh, hell. That puts a kink in things. But at least we have something to start with." Vincent ran a hand through his hair, then rolled his head from one shoulder to the other. "I'm dead tired. For some reason, I couldn't sleep last night. That sexual-assault case kept going around in my mind. I want to make sure we have enough evidence on that creep. He needs to be behind bars for the rest of his life."

"I wouldn't worry about that case. Noreen tells me that she feels confident about the evidence. I can assure you that she's not about to make any plea deals."

Noreen, the district attorney for Carson City, also happened to be his father's girlfriend, so Evan not only was acquainted with her through courthouse dealings but also saw her from time to time on the Silver Horn when she came out to have dinner with Orin. Although she had the fierce tenacity of a bulldog in the courtroom, outside it, she was a lovely dark-haired woman with a soft heart. She'd changed Orin's life for the better, and no one in the family cared one whit that she was nearly twenty years younger.

Vincent left his chair and went over to a tiny table jammed between a pair of tall file cabinets and filled a foam cup with coffee from a stainless-steel percolator. Behind him, Evan warned, "That stuff is so old it's turned into black licorice. Why don't you make a new pot?"

"Why don't you?" Vincent countered. "You've been lounging around here in the office all day."

"Yeah," Evan said with good-humored sarcasm. "I spend every day lounging around the office wondering if I'm going to enjoy my retirement as much as Granddad."

"Never. Your granddad has a lovely wife to keep him company. When you get old, you're going to be alone with nothing but a TV to stare at."

"Look who's talking about a wife. You divorced yours."

Vincent took a sip of the coffee, then made a sour face. "No. She divorced me. I wasn't home enough to suit her."

Both men were well aware that Vincent had divorced his wife because she'd become an alcoholic and had refused to get help. But Evan never reminded his partner of that fact. Vincent had already suffered more than any man should have over the breakup of his marriage. Evan wasn't about to pour salt into the wound.

"So is your dad still seeing Noreen?" Vincent asked as he returned to the chair at his desk.

Evan nodded. "Their relationship appears to be strong and steady."

"So he's not a bit worried that she might be after his money?"

Knowing he was talking about Bianca, Evan leveled a pointed look at him. "No. But not all women are like my ex-fiancée."

Vincent clapped his hands loudly. "Hallelujah. You're finally seeing the light."

Was he? Ever since Evan had left Noelle's house the other night, he'd not been able to see anything but her. He'd not been able to think of anything but her. She'd given up a husband and riches to live a life that would be best for her. And now, after four years, she said she was happier for it. But would she always feel that way? After a while, would she start regretting her choice to give up all that wealth? Would she get tired of working herself weary with very little to show for it and decide to head back to Arizona?

If that ever happened, he'd be left out in the cold.

You're going to be left out in the cold anyway, Evan. If you don't think so, just remember how she ran away from your kiss and left you standing at the door like a frozen idiot.

The voice in Evan's head was suddenly interrupted by Vincent's.

"Evan, that's your phone, not mine. Are you waiting on me to get up and answer it for you?"

Cursing under his breath, Evan reached for the phone on his desk and was surprised to hear his half sister, Sassy, on the other end of the line.

"Hi, Evan. I hope I'm not interrupting anything important. I tried your cell, but the connection kept dropping."

"Don't worry about it," he assured her. "Everything

is quiet at the moment. How are you and the baby doing?"

"My belly is bigger than a giant pumpkin now," she joked. "But seriously, we're both doing okay. Only three more months to go, and you'll be an uncle again."

Evan smiled at the thought. Sassy and Jett's three-year-old son, J.J., was quite a rounder. But for some unexplainable reason, the boy was all polite manners whenever Evan appeared on the scene. Everyone in the family had laughingly accused Evan of threatening the little imp with jail time.

"So you and Jett don't know the sex of the baby yet?"

"Oh, no! We didn't know with J.J., and that's the way we want it with this one. We'll know whenever it arrives," she told him happily. "Now I'd better get to the point before you get sidetracked with work. I'm calling to invite you to our Christmas party. It's a week from Friday night at seven. Can you make it? Dad and Noreen are coming. And our brothers are, too."

"Sure. I'll do my best. Do I need to bring anything? Other than gifts and myself," he added with a wry chuckle.

"Don't bring gifts or food. But it would be great if you'd bring a date."

"A date! Pregnancy has done something to your thinking, girl! What gave you the idea I'd bring a woman to the party?"

Out of the corner of his eye, he could see Vincent's head fly up. No doubt the word *date* had caught his attention. Except for his outing with Noelle the other day, Evan hadn't taken a woman anywhere in months and months. Oh, for a while after he'd broken up with Bianca, he'd tried to get back into the dating scene, but nothing about it had given him any pleasure, and he'd given up. Still, Vincent was always trying to set him up on a blind date, even though Evan continued to balk at the idea.

"It's the Christmas season," Sassy said. "The time when miracles happen. And I can hope, can't I?"

"It would take a miracle, all right," Evan muttered.

"Well, Dad says you took someone to see your grand-parents the other day. Why don't you invite her?"

Evan turned his chair so that Vincent couldn't see his face. "Noelle?"

"Well, yes," Sassy answered. "Isn't she the woman who saved your life?"

Unconsciously, Evan's fingers rose to the fresh scar above his ear. Noelle had done more than save his life. She'd jerked a few scales from his eyes. Even so, he wasn't at all sure he should get involved with her. Hell, he wasn't even sure she'd let him pursue her in a roman-tic way. Not after she'd run from his kiss like a rabbit from a fox. And what if she did allow him to pursue her? Would he want something lasting to come of it? He'd been so wrong about Bianca, he wasn't sure he could trust his judgment about women anymore.

"Yes, but— Never mind. I'll be there one way or the other. Now I've got to get back to work. Thanks for the invite, Sis."

"Okay. See you Friday," she said cheerily.

Swiveling the chair back toward his desk, Evan hung up the telephone while Vincent studied him with a wry expression.

"Don't you have anything better to do than to sit around eavesdropping on my phone calls?" Evan asked. "We've got a load of cases to solve!"

"Yes, sir!" Vincent snatched up a fistful of papers

from his desk. "I'll get right to work. I won't even ask you about this Noelle—whoever she is."

Thankfully, Vincent decided to go quiet, and Evan tried to resume his study of the notes he'd made on the Watson evidence. But after five minutes, his mind was still refusing to focus. All he could think about was Noelle being alone out there on those windswept hills with no one to help her do anything, much less celebrate her birthday and Christmas.

With a groan, Evan left his desk and reached for the jacket and hat he'd left hanging on a coat rack.

"Where are you going?"

Evan levered his Stetson onto his head. "I have something to do. I won't be long."

"You don't need your partner to help you?"

"Not this time. This is personal."

Later that evening, shortly before dark, Noelle had just finished her chores and was at the barn unsaddling Lonesome when she heard a vehicle approaching.

Curious about who it might be, she balanced the weight of the saddle on her hip and turned to gaze toward the house. The sight of Evan's truck rolling to a stop in the front yard pushed her heart into a rapid rhythm. She'd never expected to see him again. What was he doing here?

Her mind whirling with questions, she put the saddle in the tack room and left the barn. By the time she'd walked up the hill to the house, Evan was at the front door, holding a huge red poinsettia. The sight of him and the festive plant was like a dose of warm sun after a long, cold winter.

"The door is open," she told him. "Go on in."

At the sound of her voice, he whirled around to see her standing a few feet behind him.

Smiling, he asked, "Where did you come from?"

"The barn. If I'd been a bear, you would've been in trouble."

To her surprise, his expression turned sheepish. "I'm probably already in trouble with you."

She crossed the few feet of bare dirt until she was standing next to him at the door. It was all she could do to stop herself from looping her arm through his and jerking him into the house. He smelled so wonderful. Like a clean mountain meadow full of grass and sunshine. And the apologetic grin on his face warmed the cold, lonely spots inside her.

Stepping around him, she opened the front door and gestured for him to enter. "What makes you think you'd be in trouble with me?"

"I haven't called or been around."

She followed him into the house, then turned and shut the door behind her. "You never promised to call or come. I wasn't expecting to hear from you or see you." But she'd been hoping, she thought. Hoping far too much.

"Well, you didn't exactly give me a chance to promise anything."

"I know. And I'm sorry about that, Evan," she said ruefully. "I wasn't running away from you. But I guess it looked like that, didn't it?"

"Pretty much. But I didn't come here to talk about that." He handed the plant to her. After she'd taken it, he pulled another long box from beneath his arm and waved it at her. "I thought you needed the flower to make the house look like Christmas. And this is to give you energy."

Laughing, she placed the beautiful poinsettia on the coffee table. "Energy? I realize I look tired, but I didn't know it was that bad."

"You don't look tired," he corrected her. "But I figure with all the work you do, you must be."

Shaking her head, she accepted the box from him and opened the lid to reveal several rows of fancy chocolate candies.

"Oh, yum. I've been building fence all afternoon. I think I can afford to eat at least three." She carried the box over to the couch and sat down. "Want to join me?"

He eased out of his jacket, then placed it over the arm of a chair and added his hat on top. As Noelle watched his easy movements, she was reminded of how it had felt to be crushed against his rock-hard muscles and have his mouth consuming hers. After she'd been hurt and deceived by Phillip, she'd believed she'd never be able to feel passion again. She'd never met another man she wanted to sit next to, much less kiss. Having Evan wake up all that sleeping desire had left her both stunned and worried.

Sitting beside her, he rested his arm across the back of the couch behind her. "Don't tell me you build fence, too. I thought you told me you hired hands from the Double X when you needed extra work done."

"I do hire them when it's time to work the whole herd with vaccinations and castrating. Building fence isn't what I consider extra work. It's a fairly frequent chore. And I'd been putting off repairing that stretch of fence over by the gulch, the one you crossed over on Lonesome the day of your accident."

His eyes suddenly went dark and narrow. "You've been way out there today? Fixing fence?"

Confused by his reaction, she shrugged. "That's

right. I'm a long way from finished. There was more of it down than I thought. But if the snow holds off, I should get most of it done in the next few days."

He took the box of candy from her lap and placed it on the coffee table, then reached over and pressed her hand between his.

"I'd rather you didn't, Noelle."

Frowning, she shook her head. "Listen, Evan. I'm a big, strong girl. I know how to dig a posthole and stretch wire. I learned that from my uncle Rob years ago. It's no big deal."

"That's not the problem. I'm concerned about you being out there alone. Remember? I told you the body we discovered was only a mile or a little more from the gulch."

"He didn't die on my property."

"We're not sure where he died, exactly," Evan informed her. "We know only where his body was dumped after he was dead. That's what I was doing the day you found me—trying to figure out what direction the killer had come from and why he'd chosen that spot."

"Killer? Body dumped? So it was a homicide," she said with surprise. "What happened to him? Or are you allowed to say?"

"I'm sure the cause of death will be released at some point in the future. And I don't expect you'd be repeating whatever I say to anyone else."

Frowning, she said, "Other than Jessi at the Grubstake or my neighbor to the south, I don't do much chatting. And even if I did, I don't reveal things that are said to me in confidence."

"You have a neighbor to the south? How far from here?"

"Oh, maybe five miles. Bernice Stivers. She's seventy-five. Her husband died about six years ago. She lives alone now. But she's in good enough health to take care of herself, and she has a nephew who comes by frequently to check on her. Or so she says. I've never seen the guy. Why? What does my neighbor have to do with all this?"

"Nothing. I just wasn't aware there was another house near here. Mrs. Stivers must be over in Douglas County, otherwise I would've already questioned her."

"I believe her place is in Douglas County. But I'm not sure. I rarely ever drive over in that direction."

He stared thoughtfully at a spot across the room before he finally turned his gaze back to hers. "Sorry, Noelle. I was just trying to piece a few things together. As for the victim, he died from being injected with a lethal dose of bute."

Noelle's mouth fell open. "Are you talking about phenylbutazone?"

Evan nodded. "That's exactly what I'm talking about."

"Oh, my. I have a bottle of that stored away in the kitchen. The vet prescribed it for Driller when he hurt his ankle. Now you're going to get the notion that I could be a murderer."

"Why on earth would I think that?"

Realizing how ridiculous she sounded, she glanced away from his probing gaze. "Well, you are a lawman first and foremost. Just because I have some of the drug, you could be thinking I found a trespasser on my land and got so angry that I shot him full of the stuff."

Squeezing her hand, he let out a short laugh. "You really should try your hand at writing fiction, Noelle. You have quite an imagination."

She'd not had an imagination before Andy had been

shot by that policeman. But after her brother's senseless death, it was easy for her to picture a lawman jumping to the wrong conclusions. Until she'd met this man sitting close to her side. Evan was doing something to the confusion and hate and resentment she'd been carrying around for all these years. He was forcing her to ask herself exactly why Andy had wound up in that deadly situation in the first place. A lawman certainly hadn't forced him to ride around with a car full of criminals who'd already been in and out of the court system.

Clearing her throat, she said, "Sorry. Please finish the rest of your thought."

"What I'm concerned about, Noelle, is that you live on this isolated ranch with no one else around. Right now I'm only guessing, but I have a gut feeling the crime might be related to cattle rustling. If it is, you could be a vulnerable target."

An uneasy shiver rippled down her spine, and she rose and walked across the room. She rarely ever worried over her own safety, but when it came to her cattle, that was another thing. "Damn it, Evan, is this the only reason you came out here tonight? When I first saw you with the flower, I was—well, I was happy. Now I think all you wanted was to scare me with this stuff that has no bearing on me."

With her back to him, she didn't know he was anywhere near until his hands closed around her upper arms. She sighed as he pulled her back against him and pressed his lips to the top of her head.

"Forgive me, Noelle. I didn't mean to get carried away. None of that is why I'm here. I wanted to see you. I wanted to tell you how much I've missed you these past few days. And I wanted to invite you to drive into town with me tonight and watch the Christmas parade."

Her heart was suddenly spilling over with emotions that had no rhyme or reason. She knew only that whatever she felt was warm and wonderful, and she never wanted it to end.

Turning to face him, she rested her hands against the middle of his white shirt. The fabric was stiff with starch, but the barrier couldn't prevent the warmth of his chest from permeating right through to her fingers.

"Really?" she asked.

He smiled. "Really. Why does that surprise you?"

She let out a long breath. "Everything about you surprises me, Evan. After the other night, I didn't think I'd ever see you again. I was afraid everything I'd told you about myself had put you off."

Groaning, he cradled her head against his chest and stroked his fingers through her hair. "Oh, Noelle, I've been telling myself that I should forget you. That I don't want to get serious about you. And that you don't want to get serious about me. I've even been trying to tell myself those kisses we shared meant nothing. But it hasn't worked. I want the chance to be with you. I think we deserve to give each other a try. Don't you?"

Her throat too thick to speak, she rose up on tiptoes and answered his question with a hungry kiss.

Once their lips finally parted, Evan murmured, "If you keep this up, I'm going to forget all about the Christmas parade."

Laughing softly, she pulled away from him. "Then I'd better go change clothes so we can be going." She started out of the room and tossed impishly over her shoulder, "I'll hurry."

She'd hurry back to the first real joy she'd felt in a long, long time, she thought. And deal with her worries tomorrow.

Chapter Eight

By the time Evan and Noelle arrived in town, the night had turned very cold, but the weather hadn't discouraged a large crowd from gathering along the streets. Evan found a parking spot two blocks over from the parade route, and they walked the distance until they reached the sidewalks crammed with people young and old.

Eventually, they found a place to stand where both of them had a decent view of the street. As Noelle sidled close to Evan, she looked up at him with excitement.

"I can't remember the last time I saw a parade. I'd almost forgotten the anticipation that hangs over the crowd. Can you feel it?"

Even though his arm was already wound tightly around her waist, he somehow managed to pull her even closer. Bending his head to her ear, he said, "I can feel how good it is to have you next to me."

This man was making her feel like a vixen. Something about the touch of his hand and the warm, husky sound of his voice reminded her what it was like to flirt with a man and invite him to make love to her.

Flashing him a wicked little grin, she said, "You're here to watch bands and floats and see Santa Claus. Remember?"

"Oh. How could I have forgotten that?" he teased her.

She was about to give him a playful reply when a siren sounded in the distance. A group of nearby kids began to jump and shout with eagerness.

"Here it comes," Evan announced. "Can you see? Or do I need to set you on my shoulders?"

She rolled her eyes at him. "Listen, Detective Calhoun, I've already taken you to the emergency room once. I don't want to have to take you again with a broken back."

He laughed loudly and then once again lowered his mouth to her ear. "I think I'm going to have to show you that I'm not a weakling."

The suggestive tone in his voice left no doubt where his thoughts were heading. Suddenly, after all the years, the idea of being intimate with a man seemed good and natural. Yet at the same time, she couldn't stop herself from wondering how she would feel when everything ended and they'd gone their separate ways.

Don't think about that tonight, Noelle. Just think about the pleasure of being with Evan and let the rest take care of itself.

"Maybe I ought to show you that I'm not an Amazon," she murmured.

He said nothing to that, but the smile on his face was full of promises.

For the next half hour, they watched school marching bands playing Christmas songs, floats representing local businesses and charities, and a large group of horses and riders. Finally, at the end of the procession, Santa and several elves appeared riding in a sleigh pulled by four white burros.

As the sleigh passed by Evan and Noelle, the elves showered the onlookers with pieces of wrapped candy.

Laughing, Evan helped her scoop some up and stuff them into her pocket.

"The horses will love the peppermints," she told him. "I'll share the other flavors with you."

"I have a better idea." Grabbing her hand, he led her out of the crowd. "Now that the parade has ended, let's go eat supper."

He took her to a tiny Mexican café on the outskirts of town. After a simple meal of tamales and rice, they headed back to Noelle's place.

Once he stopped the truck in front of the house, he cut the motor and turned toward her. In the dim glow of the dashboard lights, he could see her studying him with soft, watchful eyes.

"If you don't invite me in tonight, you're going to see a grown man cry," he murmured.

A tiny smile tilted the corners of her mouth, and it was all Evan could do to keep from groaning. Just looking at her lips made him hungry, made him forget that she was still trying to get over being hurt and disillusioned by a man she'd loved and trusted.

"I can't bear the thought of that," she said. "Come on and we'll dive into that box of chocolates."

Inside the house, Evan took off his jacket and hat while Noelle removed her own coat. As she headed out of the room, she said, "I'll be in the kitchen making coffee."

After he'd put his things on an armchair and run a hand through his flattened hair, he plucked up the box of chocolates from the coffee table and carried it to the kitchen. As he looked around the quiet room, he noticed there were no dishes piled in the sink tonight. Everything was neat and in its place.

Probably because she hadn't done any cooking and eating today, he thought wryly. She'd been out by that damned gulch repairing the fence. But there was little he could do about that. She was the epitome of an independent woman. He couldn't tell her what to do or where to go on her own ranch.

That thought and what it meant to him was still rolling around in his head when she entered the room and walked straight over to the coffeepot.

Before she had a chance to pop in a filter, he said, "You don't have to make that especially for me."

Her brows arched in question. "Aren't you staying long enough to drink a cup?"

Leaving the box of treats on the table, he strode over and rested his hands on her shoulders. "I'm not leaving anytime soon. I'm just not wanting coffee or candy. I'm wanting...you."

The sharp intake of her breath told him that he'd shocked her with his bluntness, but he didn't understand why his feelings had come as a surprise to her. The moment she'd kissed him, he'd known something had changed in her. Instead of snatching at what she thought she shouldn't have, her kiss had been confident and full of promises. And all evening long, he'd been feeling the electricity building between them. Now desire hummed inside him like an overloaded power line.

She tilted her head back to look at him. The movement caused her long, brown hair to fall over his hands. He instinctively snared a few silky strands with his fingers, lifted them to his nose and inhaled the fragrance.

"Evan, I—"

"Don't tell me that I've surprised you. We're adults, not teenagers. I'm fairly sure that you've been feeling the same thing I've been feeling all evening. At least, that's the message I've been getting."

She closed her eyes, and Evan had to fight to keep from lowering his mouth to hers and putting a delicious end to all this talk.

"I haven't been sending you a message."

He didn't say anything to that. His silence prompted her eyes to open and her gaze to meet his.

"Well, okay…I guess…I have been telling you in so many ways that I want you," she admitted. "But I—"

"Now that we're alone, you're getting cold feet?" he finished for her.

A torn expression crossed her face. "Not cold feet. I…" Her words trailed away. Then suddenly her arms were sliding around his waist, urging him to close the gap between their bodies. "I haven't been with a man since my ex-husband. After Phillip, the thought of being intimate with any man always left me sick inside. But you—I don't know what it is about you, Evan, but you've made me want to be a woman again. I'm just not sure that I know how anymore."

Her confession shot a bittersweet arrow right through his heart. "Oh, Noelle. Sweetheart." Reaching for her hand, he lifted it to his lips. "There are more womanly cells in one of your little fingers than in any whole female I've ever met."

She groaned. "I don't want sweet talk from you, Evan. I'd rather have straight talk."

Realizing she'd been conned by a jerk in the worst kind of way, he understood how important it was for her to know whether the things he said to her were genuine or spoken to play on her emotions.

"That's the truth," he said. "And here's the rest of it. I have no idea where any of this might take us. We might decide we don't like each other after all. Or we might decide we'll be together for a long, long time. Either way, I want to find out. Don't you?"

A part of him expected her hands to fall away from his back. Instead, he was thrilled to feel them tighten.

"No promises to give me a life in paradise? Or vows to love me until the end of time?" she asked sardonically.

If he hadn't known how hurt she'd been by her ex-husband, the tone of her voice would've had him turning and walking out of the house. But Evan understood she wasn't really a hard-hearted woman. It was the pain inside that made her hide behind a wall of sarcasm.

"I can't make those sorts of promises," he said. "Not yet, at least."

Pressing her cheek to his chest, she murmured, "I wouldn't ever want you to make those sorts of promises to me. Those are the kinds that are always broken."

"Always?"

Tilting her head back, she looked at him, and Evan didn't miss the smoky allure in her brown eyes. "That's been my experience. I can't see why yours would be any different."

Touching her face, he moved his fingertips over her high cheekbones, down her straight nose, then on to the plush, velvety curves of her lips.

"You talk tough, Noelle," he whispered. "But you don't feel a bit tough to me."

Something soft and needy flickered in her eyes. Her hands began to move against his back, creating sizzling patches of heat across his skin.

"Right now, I think you're talking too much." Her voice was hoarse with desire, and the sound of it ruined

Evan's plan for them to take things slowly and safely and thoughtfully.

Without another word, he slipped one arm beneath her thighs and lifted her up to his chest.

"Evan!" Gasping, she flung her arms around his neck. "I'm too heavy for this!"

He chuckled at her panicked protest and started out of the room. "Like I told you at the parade, you need to see I'm not a weakling."

Other than the kitchen, living area and bathroom, there were only two other rooms in the house, and it was easy for Evan to find which bedroom she slept in. A tiny night lamp illuminated a portion of the bed with an arc of muted light. He carried her straight to the bed, but as soon as he deposited her on the worn patchwork quilt, her upper body popped straight up.

"My boots are dirty. Let me—"

"I'll take care of your boots," he interrupted her in an urgent rush. "I'll take care of everything."

Pushing her back against the mattress, he pulled off her scarred cowboy boots and tossed them aside. But the moment he started to remove her clothing, he forced himself to slow and his hands to calm.

Except for the ticking of an old bell alarm clock on the nightstand, the room was incredibly quiet. He could hear each breath she took, and between the rapid intakes, his heartbeat was pounding in his ears, adding its own rhythm to the sounds.

He had yet to kiss her or touch her bare skin, but his body was already aroused to the painful point. The realization shocked him. He couldn't remember wanting any woman this much. Just thinking about being inside her was nearly enough to send him over the edge.

The fight to contain his desire was making his hands

shake. He fumbled with the top button on her blouse, then the second and third, until Noelle let out an impatient groan and attempted to push his fingers aside.

"I can do this much faster," she told him.

Evan carefully placed her hands above her head. "Faster isn't always better," he said, his voice thick.

Lifting her hands to his head, she pushed her fingers through his hair and shoved them down to the scalp. "Don't worry. If you stick to this pace, we'll soon be hearing the rooster crow."

Laughing softly, he dropped his lips to the bared skin above her lacy bra. "Funny, Noelle. I didn't know you had a rooster. And I sure don't know whether I should feel insulted or flattered by that remark."

With each word he spoke, he moved the tip of his nose against her creamy, soft skin and allowed the scent of her to fill his nostrils and his senses. At the same time, his hands worked to push her blouse over her shoulders.

"You should feel— Oh, my, Evan—you've convinced me," she whispered as she arched her back to allow him access to the clasp on her bra. "Slow is nice. Very nice."

The skimpy black garment fell away from her breasts. After he tossed it aside, he cupped the full mounds with his hands while his tongue lathed first one nipple and then the other until the sensitive flesh puckered into hard little buds.

"You taste too good, Elle. Too sweet and precious. Just like I knew you would." His voice sounded so hoarse that he hardly recognized it as his own. But then, nothing about the way he was feeling and reacting to this woman was familiar to him. It was as if she'd turned him into an animal filled with the primal need to mate. And if he didn't make her his own, something inside him would wither and die.

Eventually he moved away from her breasts long enough to take off the remainder of her clothing and then deal with his own. He was standing at the side of the bed, stripped down to his boxer shorts, when it suddenly dawned on him that he wasn't carrying any condoms with him. The reality was like a cold dose of water.

"What's wrong, Evan? Is the idea of having sex with me turning you into an icicle?"

She was teasing, but he couldn't find anything amusing in having to walk away from her bed. He sure as hell didn't figure she kept a box of protection in her medicine cabinet.

"I—uh—wasn't planning on anything like this happening," he finally said. "And it's rather embarrassing, but I—well, I don't have any protection with me. You know. Birth control."

She must have sensed that he was finding it awkward to bring up the subject, because an understanding smile crossed her face. Then, reaching up, she caught his hand and tugged him down beside her.

"Forget that. I'm on the Pill," she murmured against his lips. "All we need is each other."

A breath of relief rushed out of him, while hot desire rushed to his loins and tightened them in a viselike grip.

"Each other," he whispered in agreement. "Yes, that's all we need."

He closed the last fraction of an inch between their lips. For the next few moments, he kissed her deeply, hungrily, until the room around them was a spinning blur and nothing mattered except the incredible need to connect his body to hers.

The same wild desperation must have been building in her, because she suddenly tore away from the kiss and rose to her knees. When her fingers dived beneath the band of his boxer shorts, he knew her needs had grown to equal his. He lifted his hips from the bed to allow her to remove the last barrier of fabric between them.

Her hands moved urgently as she slipped the shorts down his legs and onto the floor. Then, lying on her side, face-to-face with him, she slipped her hand over his chest and down his belly until she was touching his erection. The instant her fingers wrapped around him, he couldn't stop his groan.

Pausing, she whispered sexily, "Am I hurting you?"

"No. You're killing me!" Panting, he caught her wrist and gently placed her hand aside. "I can't hold back with you touching me like that."

She nuzzled his cheek, her lips lingering at the corner of his. "Mmm. I don't want you to hold back. We have all night, don't we?"

All night? Oh, yes, it would take all night and many more to quench the lust this woman had built in him, Evan thought.

"And I don't want to waste a second of it," he murmured. Rolling her onto her back, he brought his lips down on hers and kissed her until her fingers were digging into his shoulders, her hips arching desperately up to his.

His temples pounding, his body on the verge of exploding, he finally ended the kiss and set his mouth on a downward path, between her breasts and past her navel. By the time he reached the juncture of her thighs, she was making little noises in her throat, and the needy sounds pushed him to a place he'd never been before.

Her legs parted, and he took his time tasting the soft

skin of her inner thighs, drinking in the essence of her womanly scent. His tongue finally slipped between the intimate folds, and he could think only that she was like a flower with a sweet, sweet center, beckoning him to taste and drink his fill.

When he began to feel her tighten and her breathing turn to harsh rasps, he brought his head up and quickly positioned his body over hers.

"Oh, Evan—I—I'm aching! Love me—love me!"

Her desperate plea ripped through him like a burst of blinding light. As he drove himself into her hot body, he was consumed by a wave of emotion. It swelled his chest and drowned his senses to the point that he was battling to stay afloat. And then suddenly, it didn't matter if he surrendered to the chaos inside him. He didn't care if he allowed her to view a part of him that no one else had seen before. As long as she rode out this emotional storm with him, he could survive anything.

Like a wild wind blowing faster and faster across the desert hills, they moved together, all the while climbing, climbing, until Evan was certain his heart was going to burst wide-open and his lungs burn in the aftermath.

Beneath him, she was all heat and softness, melding and blending with his body as though she'd been made especially for him. Oh, yes, she fit him, he thought. She touched him in all the ways a man needed and wanted to be touched. Without even asking, she was taking something from him that couldn't be defined or measured.

"Noelle—Elle. My sweetheart."

The words came out between fierce gasps. As he mindlessly drove himself into her, she slipped a hand behind his head and tugged his mouth down to hers. The intimate connection was all it took to send him spiraling headlong into a dark, magical place where he was lost in a whirl of sensations so incredible that he couldn't breathe or think. All he could do was hang on to Noelle's slick body. As he waited for his world to stop spinning, he realized just what it was she'd been snatching from him with each and every kiss, each caress of her hands. She'd been taking bits and pieces of his heart.

Several moments passed before Noelle's heart slowed and her breathing returned to normal. By then, Evan had rolled his weight away from her. Now he lay next to her, his arms resting on the pillow behind his head. The faint glow of the night-light bathed his rugged features. As her eyes wandered over his strong, straight nose and the arrogant thrust of his chin, she wondered what had just happened to her.

The moment their bodies had connected, she'd lost every last ounce of self-control. He'd made her feel things she'd never felt before. He'd made her ache with want and then given her everything she'd asked for and more.

Now there was a soft radiance warming her from the inside out, pushing away the long, lonely years she'd endured since she'd moved onto this piece of land. Yet somewhere among all the tender thoughts she was having about this man, a part of her was remembering that he was wealthy by birth and a lawman by choice.

Up until a few days ago, Andy's picture had sat on her nightstand for the past five years. But after she'd shown Evan the album of wedding photos, something had told her to store the image of Andy away. That it was time she move on and put the incident behind her.

Now she could only wonder what her little brother would think if he'd known his sister had made love to a man who wore a badge and carried a gun. Would he think she'd betrayed him? That she'd deserted him in death the same way she'd let him down while he'd been alive?

Before she could let herself dwell on that somber question, Evan stirred beside her. As he reached over and drew her to him, she refused to let anything ruin this special night. Tomorrow would be soon enough for her to feel guilty. Tonight she simply wanted to feel loved and needed.

Pillowing her cheek against his shoulder, she wrapped her arm around his chest and snuggled close to his side. "I saw Jessi at the Grubstake this morning. She tried her best to talk me into going to the Christmas parade with her tonight. When I told her no, she practically got angry with me. She thinks I ought to get out and have more fun. She doesn't understand what makes me happy."

His fingers gently stroked the damp hair clinging to her temples. "What does make you happy?" he asked drowsily. "Riding Driller or Lonesome?"

"I do love my horses." Smiling faintly, she used her forefinger to draw lazy looping figures across his chest. "I didn't think having you here with me like this would make me happy, but it does."

His hand rested against her back. "It makes me happy, too."

Tilting her head, she flashed a glance at his face. "Does it really?"

"More than it should."

Sighing, she rose on her elbow and gazed down at him. He was being far more pensive than she'd thought he would be, and that worried her. Having sex with this man was one thing, but what would she do if he actually got serious about her? How could she explain that Andy's death had skewed everything she'd ever thought or imagined a man of the law to be? Her bitterness would no doubt squash any feelings Evan might have for her. And God help her, as much as she wanted to forgive and forget the cause of her brother's senseless death, she couldn't.

Swallowing at the thickness in her throat, she said, "You sound like you regret what just happened between us. Why?"

"I don't regret anything. But I'm wondering where this is going to take us. Whatever you might think, I'm not a man who jumps into a woman's bed just for the fun of it."

"And I've already told you that I haven't slept with a man since my ex-husband. But why should we worry about any of that or where this might lead us?" she countered. "Isn't it enough that we can simply enjoy each other's company?"

His fingertips stroked her cheekbone. "You're right. There's no need for us to be serious or worried. We're just now getting to know each other. And tonight we've gotten off to a good start, don't you think?"

"The best," she whispered. Then, closing her eyes, she lowered her lips to his. When he deepened the kiss and her body began to burn with desire once again, she tried to forget that this time with him had to be short-lived.

Because no matter how wonderful this man made her feel, in the long term, she couldn't let herself fall in love with a lawman.

Chapter Nine

A week later, on Tuesday afternoon, Noelle was back out at the gulch, slamming the posthole digger into the hard earth. Five more holes to dig and then she'd be able to set the last of the cedar posts she needed to reach the boundary fence that ran alongside the country road. The work was slow and exhausting, but she was proud of the progress she'd made. With the fence completely repaired, there would be no chance of any stray cattle wandering onto her land.

She was leaning on the posthole digger, catching her breath, when she heard a vehicle approaching and glanced around to see Evan's truck pulling to the side of the blacktop road. Even though he'd spent the past three nights with her, the sight of him sent a thrill of joy through her.

While he left the truck and ducked under the barbed-wire fence, Noelle left the digger propped in the shallow hole and walked through the dead grass and sagebrush to meet him.

As soon as she reached his side, he bent his head and placed a swift kiss on her lips.

"Mmm. That's a nice greeting," she said with a smile. "What are you doing out here so early? I thought you wouldn't be off duty until later tonight."

He grimaced. "I'm not off duty. But since I was in

the vicinity, I thought I'd drive by. I had an idea you might be working on the fence."

Since the other night when he'd expressed his concern about her being alone near the gulch, he hadn't said anything more about it. She supposed he'd come to the conclusion that she needed to deal with her work in her own way, and he had no right to interfere.

"It's nearly finished. Five more posts and then stretching the last of the wire. Why don't you come have a look at my handiwork? I think you'll be proud of me."

Curling her arm through his, she urged him forward.

As they strolled toward the spot where she'd been working, he asked, "You've not seen any stray cattle around, have you?"

"No. My herd is grazing in a little valley two hills to the west of here. I haven't seen any cattle on the land that joins mine. As a matter of fact, the neighboring ranch has been empty for as long as I've lived here. That's why I wasn't too concerned with the downed fence until you rode over it," she added with a pointed smile. "Why are you asking about cattle?"

"In the past day or two, another small herd over in Douglas County has disappeared. Before the rustlers can haul them to market, they'll have to dump the stolen cattle somewhere until they can change the identifying ear tags or try to burn another brand over the old one."

The smile fell from her face. "And what makes you think they would dump them here, by me?"

"You're not far from the county line." He pointed in the direction of his parked truck. "And this road that runs by your property probably doesn't see four or five cars in a day's time. Isn't that about right?"

"Yes, but there are plenty of other isolated roads around here." She gave him a curious glance. These past few nights they'd been together, he hadn't talked about his work. But then, talking hadn't exactly been on either of their minds. They'd spent most of the time in her bed, and the heat of those moments was still so fresh in her mind that just thinking about it made her want to pull him down right there on the dead grama grass.

"Are you still thinking the stolen cattle has something to do with that man's death?"

"That notion is just a hunch. But I did run the idea by my partner. He's not convinced. He won't rule it out, either." Evan shook his head. "That's enough about that, though. Let's have a look at this fence you're building."

The two of them moved down the fence line until they reached the area where she'd already strung the barbed wire and fastened it to the cedar posts with staples. After giving the taut wire a pluck, he looked at her.

"I'm impressed. Everything is straight and tight." He gestured to a long-handled device lying nearby on the ground. "I hope you're being careful with that wire stretcher. They're dangerous to use."

"I know. I've been lashed with barbed wire before." She pointed to a spot on her upper thigh. "I had to have several stitches."

"Oh. I wondered what had caused that scar." Shaking his head with dismay, he reached for her hand and pressed it tightly between his. "Noelle, don't you know that I'd be more than happy to help you with this?"

"It's sweet of you to offer, Evan. But you can't take off work to help me with this sort of thing. And I don't expect you to."

"I didn't mean I'd personally help you. I'd hire someone to do it for you."

His words left her colder than the brisk north wind. With her lips pressed tightly together, she moved away from his side and headed toward the spot where she'd left the posthole digger. Evan walked along beside her.

"I don't want or need financial aid from you," she said stiffly.

He blew out a heavy breath. "I'm not trying to insult you, Noelle. I'm trying to help you."

She halted in her tracks and turned to him. "You know, for a moment back there, I was very touched that you offered to help. Your willingness to work by my side was such a nice thought. One that I truly appreciated. I should've known you consider yourself above doing manual work like this."

"I hardly think I deserve that comment from you," he shot back at her. "If you're implying that I'm unused to getting my hands dirty with ranch work, then you're all wrong!"

"Am I?" she countered. "Maybe I should ask your family about that."

His face went red, and Noelle was suddenly ashamed of her outburst.

"Sorry. I shouldn't have said that," she murmured with regret. "I guess I'm a little sensitive when it comes to men and money."

"Only a little?"

She had to chuckle, and the sound broke the tension between them. "Okay. I misconstrued your offer. But I—"

Before she could finish, he reached for her gloved hands and drew her to his chest. "I'm sorry, too. None of what I said came out right. I would like to help you do this kind of work. But you'd have to wait until I can get time off. That's why hiring a man to help makes more sense."

"But, Evan, that's not the kind of help I want from you."

He cupped his hand around her cold cheek. "I'm not trying to buy your affection, Noelle. I just want to make things easier for you. You don't deserve to have bleeding blisters on your hands or your face chapped by the freezing wind."

She understood that he was trying to be kind to her. Yet he didn't realize that while he was doing it, he was making her feel like something less than a woman. "Look, Evan, I'm never going to be a fragile little woman with soft hands, pretty skin and immaculate makeup. Heck, I rarely ever have any reason to wear a dress. Maybe you—" she looked away from him and swallowed as emotions suddenly choked her "—ought to find a better woman than me. One who is feminine and needy and—"

Suddenly his cheek was pressed to hers, and his arms were crushing her tightly against him. His warm embrace flooded Noelle's eyes with moisture. She blinked in a furious effort to keep the tears from brimming onto her cheeks.

"I don't need to look anywhere but right here at you, Elle. You're the woman I want."

Was she? These past few days, he'd made love to her as though she was the most precious thing on earth to him. But in the light of day, when they were apart, cool reality kept slipping in, reminding her that what had started out as one night of pleasure had snowballed out of control and into something far bigger than she'd imagined. And she'd stood silently by and let it all happen. Because she wanted him. Because for the first time in years, she had something more than her little ranch to think about, to care about. But she couldn't let it continue. Not without first explaining her feelings. And after that, she was fairly certain whatever this thing was budding between them would be crushed dead.

"I think…we need to talk, Evan. Are you coming out tonight after work?"

Easing her back, his eyes narrowed skeptically as he studied her face. "Yes. I don't know what time exactly, but I'll be here. What should we talk about? If this is about us, then I want to discuss it now. We'll go to my truck and—"

She interrupted him with a shake of her head. "No. Now isn't the time or place. I need to explain some things to you, and I don't want to do it here."

It was obvious to Noelle that he wanted to argue the point, but after a moment he relented.

"Okay. I'll be here as early as I can," he promised.

Her heart winced with dread. "I'll be waiting."

He kissed her, and the hunger she tasted on his lips made her want to weep. After he'd said goodbye, she couldn't bring herself to watch him walk away. Instead, she reached for the diggers and with all her strength slammed them into the hard dirt.

Something was definitely wrong with Noelle. This afternoon when Evan had found her out by the gulch, there had been something off in her voice. As he'd kissed her, he hadn't missed the glaze of moisture in her eyes.

Damn it, if something was bothering her, she should've told him about it right there and then. Instead, he'd spent the past few hours in agony, trying to figure out what could be going on in that pretty head of hers.

When he'd first walked up, she'd seemed perfectly happy to see him. But then he'd made that remark about hiring someone to help her, and everything from there had gone downhill in a hurry.

"Evan, are you getting sick?"

The question snapped Evan's head around to see his partner eyeing him with concern. "Sorry, Vince, you're out of luck. I think I'm going to survive."

"Couldn't prove it by me. You look awful, and you've been staring at that wall for the past twenty minutes. You find something fascinating about the plaster?"

Evan frowned at him. "I've been thinking."

"That's obvious. What about? That woman you've been seeing? Or the Watson case?"

Squinting, Evan asked, "What woman?"

Vincent batted a hand through the air. "Oh, come off it. For the past three evenings when you've left the office, you've headed south. The Silver Horn is north of here."

Picking up a pen, Evan began to doodle on a notepad. "Could be I was going out to Bonito's to eat supper."

"Why would you do that when you've told me the Silver Horn has the best cook in the whole county?"

Tossing down the pen, Evan leaned back in his chair and raked both hands through his hair. "All right. I have been seeing Noelle Barnes. Remember, she—"

"Barnes. Yeah, I remember that name now. She's the woman who helped you that day you had the horse accident. You've been seeing her? For real?"

Funny that Vincent should use the word *real*. Everything about Noelle and how Evan felt about her was probably the most real thing that had ever happened to him. He wasn't sure why or how his feelings for the woman had developed so rapidly, but it was becoming evident that she meant far more to him than just a bed partner. But that realization only filled him with more worrisome questions. She was a very independent woman, and her future was wrapped up in that little ranch of hers. He couldn't see her giving it up to make a life with him. So where would that leave the two of them?

He sighed. "For real."

"Well, she must be a true dish to catch your eye."

A dish? Noelle could hardly be described in those terms. There was nothing contrived or glamorous about her. She was simply all sexy woman, and making love to her had turned him inside out.

"I doubt you'd take a second look at her. But she's a beautiful woman to me."

The goading grin on Vincent's face disappeared. "Hey, you really mean that, don't you?"

Leaning forward in the chair, Evan rested his elbows on the desktop and looked over at his friend and co-worker. "It scares me how much I mean it, Vince. I don't understand what's happened. You know how leery I've been of dating since that fiasco with Bianca. I haven't even looked at a woman, much less gotten serious about one. And now—well, I have no idea where this thing with Noelle is headed, and it scares the hell out of me."

"Where do you want it to go?" Vincent asked. "All the way to the altar?"

Evan grimaced. "A few days ago I would've called you crazy for mentioning that word to me. But now I can't imagine the future without her in it."

"Sounds to me like you've already fallen in love with her."

Love. Was that the emotion filling him with this desperate need to protect her, to make her happy, to provide her with all the things that would make her life better?

I think we need to talk.

Noelle's remark had hardly sounded as if she wanted to pledge her love to him. So where was that going to leave him? Most likely wishing he'd never ridden Lonesome into that damned gulch. That was where.

"Let's talk about something else," Evan muttered. "Tell me what you found out about Bernice's nephew, Billy Stivers. Anything suspicious?"

Vincent picked up a notebook from his desk and began to read. "He's twenty-six. No wife or kids. As a juvenile, he committed one petty theft and was sentenced to do community service. A few months ago, he was working for Conroy Freight as a truck driver but was fired for altering his log record. Since then, according to the info I could gather from acquaintances, he's just been bumming around between the Carson City area and a friend's place in Orange County, California."

"Hmm. He could have a connection to the Watson case, but we need more than that to go on. I had a little talk with his elderly aunt this afternoon. She lives a few miles from Noelle's ranch, in fact."

Curious, Vincent walked over to Evan's desk and rested a thigh on one corner. "That's interesting. And Noelle lives not far from where you had your accident. Where you found the tire tracks leading off the road and into the desert."

"That's right. And I'll tell you something, Vince, it worries me to think of Noelle out there alone. The woman isn't scared of anything. And she'd fight tooth and nail to protect her home and livestock."

"Sounds like she needs a lawman to protect her."

Evan smiled wryly. "Maybe you can convince her of that. I can't."

Later that night, when Evan arrived at Noelle's house, she ushered him in. He was shocked to see her wearing a long black-and-beige-patterned skirt and a black turtleneck. Her hair was twisted into a bun atop her head, and she'd even put on pink lipstick. She looked so beautiful, his first urge was to lift her into his arms and carry her straight to the bedroom.

Instead, he simply kissed her cheek and drew in the soft scent of flowers clinging to her hair and skin. "You look very fetching," he murmured.

"Thank you. I thought it was about time I let you see me in something other than jeans and boots." She gestured toward the kitchen. "I have stew left over from my supper. If you're hungry, I'd be glad to heat it up for you."

"I'm fine. I had a sandwich earlier at my desk." He followed her over to the couch. "Sorry I couldn't get here earlier. We were about to wrap things up for the evening when we were called out to investigate a robbery scene."

"No worries. It's still early."

She sat down in the middle of the couch, and he joined her on the next cushion. After they were both settled, he reached for her hand.

"So what is this talk about, Elle? I've been worried all afternoon. Today at the gulch, you sounded—well, unhappy. Are you still angry with me?"

She placed her free hand over his. "I wasn't angry with you. More like disappointed. But that's not what this is about. I—"

Pausing, she glanced away, and Evan could see that some sort of turmoil was going on inside her. Then he noticed an open letter lying on the coffee table.

"Has something happened? Is that letter bad news?" he asked.

Her short laugh was brittle. "Actually, that letter is

from my parents. Sort of a Christmas/birthday card, I guess you'd call it."

"I wasn't aware that they stayed in contact with you."

She grimaced. "They don't. Not regularly. I guess they were feeling the spirit of the season, or suddenly remembered they had a child at Christmastime," she said mockingly. "They're in Paris right now, but they'll be back in Phoenix sometime after New Year's Day. They wanted to remind me that if I ever got tired of playing cowgirl, I was welcome to come home and live like a 'real' person."

Something cold hit the pit of Evan's stomach. Is that what had brought about this change in her demeanor? Had hearing from her parents gotten her thinking she wanted more than this meager life here in Nevada?

"Have you answered it yet?"

She turned an odd look on him. "I won't be answering it at all. They know I'll never be coming back. Once in a while they send me photos or letters just as a way to dig at me—to punish me for leaving and turning my back on them."

"Maybe it would help you, Noelle, if you did contact them once in a while. After all, they are your parents."

"They're thieves," she said flatly. "They cheat others so that they can live in luxury. No, Evan. I don't want any part of that."

He sighed. "My family hasn't always been a pillar of perfection," he told her. "My father and grandfather have done things I was hardly proud of. But I don't hate them for their mistakes."

"I don't hate my parents," she replied. "I guess you could say I've simply given up on them."

"Okay. So if it's not that letter, then what did you want to tell me?"

Drawing in a deep breath, she rose to her feet, picked up the letter and carried it over to the little rolltop desk. "It's about us. Well, more about me, I should say." She stuffed the letter into a small side drawer, then turned to face him. "I think—these past few days, I've been letting myself dream that you and I—that we could be happy together. At least for a while."

Unable to remain seated, he jumped to his feet and walked over to where she stood with her back resting against the edge of the desk. "I don't understand. You've seemed very happy to be with me."

She nodded, then dropped her head. "I'm not going to lie. These last few days with you have made me happier than I've ever been, but there's something you need to know about me." Lifting her head, she bravely met his gaze. "I don't like law officers. I mean, not until I met you and your grandfather."

"Oh, Elle, that doesn't come as a surprise. You more or less made that clear the night you drove me home to the Horn. I tried not to take it personally." He smiled and shook his head. "Besides, you seemed to get past all of that pretty quickly."

"I'm trying. And most of the time when I'm with you, the thought never enters my mind. But at other times, I feel very guilty and confused."

Seeing the agony in her eyes, he realized that this went far deeper than resentment over a speeding ticket or some other simple infraction of the law.

Gently rubbing his hand against her upper arm, he urged her to go on. "I can't imagine you having anything to feel guilty about. If you've had some sort of serious brushup with the law, I'll understand."

She looked at him for long, agonizing moments. Finally she said, "Five years ago, a policeman shot my brother, Andy. He died from his wounds."

Evan was stunned. No, he was more than that. He was aching for this woman who had become so important to him. "Oh. When you said that he'd died, I figured it was from a medical problem. Or an accident. Was this an accidental shooting?"

"That's the way the police department ruled it. You see, Andy had gone with a few of his friends to a convenience store not far from where they lived. He wasn't aware that they were going to commit armed robbery. At least, that's what the police inquiry reported, after it was too late. When the police arrived, Andy was— well, in the middle of the chaos, and he was shot down by one of the policemen. Ironically, his buddies were arrested, unharmed."

"What happened to the policeman who did the shooting?"

She shrugged, but he could see that there was nothing indifferent about the pain in her eyes. "He was suspended until the investigation was over, then reinstated after he was cleared of any wrongdoing."

"I see," Evan said thoughtfully. "And what did you think about the decision? That it was wrong? That justice hadn't been served in the death of your brother?"

The breath that rushed past her lips was more like a shaky sob. "Something like that. I thought someone ought to pay for taking his life. He was only eighteen."

"I think I would've been feeling the same way. Even now, if something like that happened to one of my siblings, I'm not sure I could continue working in the office. Losing a loved one like that would skew my whole way of thinking toward the law."

Surprise pushed some of the dark shadows from her eyes. "Do you really mean that?"

"Every word."

Her features crumpled with regret. "Oh, Evan, you said you didn't take it personally when I voiced my dislike of lawmen. But you should have, because I meant it personally. Up until a few weeks ago, I held a low opinion of you all. But then, when I found you in the gulch that day—when I started to get to know you—something inside me began to change. And after we visited your grandparents in Virginia City, I realized it was wrong of me to blame you for losing my brother."

As she spoke the last few words, tears began to roll down her _face. His need to console her was so deep and intense that for a moment, his throat was too choked to speak. All he could do was gather her closely and cradle her head against his shoulder.

"Oh, Elle, sweetheart, it's all going to be okay," he finally managed to whisper against the top of her head. "This isn't something that's going to come between the two of us. Not now. Not ever."

Lifting her head from his shoulder, she looked at him with wet, troubled eyes. "But it will, Evan! I—"

Before she could go on, he urged her over to the couch. "Come with me," he said gently. "You need to sit."

She allowed him to lead her back to the couch. Once they were settled and facing each other, the urge to brace her and keep her safely at his side had him reaching for both her hands.

Squeezing them tightly, he prompted her, "All right, finish what you were about to say."

"I'll try." Closing her eyes, she shook her head. "I don't know how to make you understand. But the other night—that first night we went to bed together, I—well, I wasn't expecting it to be so…special. I expected it to be a onetime thing, and I kept telling myself that it didn't matter you were a lawman. But it hasn't turned out that way. You came back."

"Didn't you want me to?"

"Yes," she whispered hoarsely. "More than you know. And that makes me feel very guilty somehow. Like I'm turning my back on my brother."

"By being with me? That doesn't make sense, Elle."

"I agree. It doesn't make any sense. I—just can't help how I feel. That's why I wanted to tell you all of this. Because it wasn't fair to keep it from you. Not if we plan to keep seeing each other."

The mere fact that she was willing to share this painful part of her life with him was a start for their future, he thought. Whatever that future might be.

"I'm glad you decided to tell me, Elle. And I'd like to hear a little about Andy. What kind of relationship did you have with him?"

He could see from the expression on her face that his question surprised her. Maybe she thought he didn't care. Maybe a part of her was still thinking of him as a shoot-first-ask-questions-later kind of lawman. The notion bothered him. But not nearly enough to walk away from her. He couldn't imagine anything bothering him that much.

"I was five years older than Andy, so there was a bit of an age gap between us. But when we were small, we were close. We had to be. Our parents were gone so much that most of the time, it was just the two of us rambling around in a huge house with nothing but a nanny, a cook and a maid. I think Andy was more affected by our parents' absence than I was. He liked sports and began playing basketball in grade school. He desperately wanted Dad to take an interest and would often beg him to come to the games."

"Did he?"

A mocking frown turned down the corners of her lips. "Oh, once in a while Dad would make a half-hearted effort to show up. But kids are smart. They know when someone isn't sincere. Anyway, by the time Andy reached high school, he'd given up on sports. He'd given up on everything, especially his parents. He drifted into a bad crowd and eventually left home."

"Did your parents try to intervene? Or get him help?"

"They sent him to a therapist. That was the easiest way to fix things, or so they thought. Neither of them realized the only way to turn Andy's life around was to invest their time and love in him." She sighed, and her troubled gaze dropped to their entwined hands. "But I'm just as guilty, Evan. I should've been a better sister. I should've tried harder to make him feel loved and wanted."

Even though Evan had seen similar situations with juveniles, he couldn't fathom the pain and worry that reverberated through the whole family when a child took the wrong track in life. Evan's parents had always been rock steady for him and his brothers. Even their crusty grandfather Bart had guided them with a love that was tough, yet sincere. It never occurred to Evan or his brothers to rebel. There'd been no reason for them to.

Releasing his hold on her hands, he reached over and stroked the curtain of brown hair away from her shoulder. "I'm sure you were a good sister."

"Not good enough."

Cupping his hand beneath her chin, he urged her gaze back to his. "You know, Elle," he said gently, "I think you blame yourself for Andy's death more than you do the policeman who mistakenly shot him."

She stared at him, and he could see a mixture of thoughts and emotions parading through her eyes.

"I've always felt guilty that I didn't do more," she said in a strained voice. "But hearing you put it in words—yes, I'm afraid you're right."

"Then don't you think it's time you forgive yourself? That you move on and allow yourself to be happy again?"

Her brown eyes searched his face for a moment longer. Then, with a little sob, she wrapped her arms around his neck and buried her face in his shoulder.

"Oh, Evan, I do want to move on—with you. If you still want me."

"Want you? Oh, sweetheart, if I want you any more, I'm going to burst wide-open."

She lifted her head from his shoulder, and her lips quivered as she tried to give him a suggestive smile. "Then maybe we should go to the bedroom, and you can show me just how much you want me. That would definitely give me a start at being happy."

With a low chuckle, he brought his lips close to hers. "I'm here to serve and protect."

She kissed him, then rose to her feet, tugging him along with her. And as she led him toward the bedroom, Evan refused to think about all she'd just told him. He refused to let himself think beyond tomorrow and the obstacles still standing between them. Right now, making love to Noelle was all that mattered.

Chapter Ten

Later that week, on Friday evening, Evan was in his bedroom getting dressed for Sassy's Christmas party when a short knock sounded on the door. His older brother strode into the room.

"Hey, Clancy. Looks like you're all ready," Evan said as he eyed his brother's tall figure dressed in jeans and boots and a fancy Western shirt. "Does Olivia feel like going tonight?"

Clancy grinned at the mention of his pregnant wife. "She's feeling great. All she can talk about is what Sassy is going to have to eat."

Sitting on the edge of the bed, Evan reached for his boots. "Well, she is eating for two now."

"Yeah. I still have to pinch myself sometimes. A few months ago, Olivia was just a memory I couldn't get over. Now she's my wife, and our baby is on the way. Sometimes it scares me to be this happy."

Even though Olivia had been pregnant before she and Clancy had gotten married, Clancy couldn't have been happier about their coming baby. "You deserve it, brother," Evan said. "You and Olivia went through some long years without each other."

Clancy walked over to the dresser and picked up a photo of their late mother, Claudia. "You know, I think

Mom would be happy with the way this family is growing. She always talked about having grandchildren."

Jerking the hem of his jeans down over the shaft of his boots, Evan glanced up at his brother. Clancy's baby would arrive in a few months, their brother Rafe already had a baby daughter, and Sassy was about to have her second child. Evan was happy for all of his siblings, though there were times he looked at them and wondered whether he would ever have the chance to be a father. He'd always wanted children and dreamed about having a family of his own, but after his engagement fell apart, he'd tried not to dwell on all the things he was missing in his life.

"I think I never really understood just what a wonderful mother Mom was until she passed away," he said.

"Mmm. I don't think people ever fully appreciate what they have until it's gone." Clancy put the photo back on the dresser and walked over to where Evan was still sitting on the edge of the bed. "Sorry, I didn't stop by to talk family. I wanted to see if you'd like to ride with me and Olivia over to Sassy and Jett's. We'd be glad to have your company, and there's no need for you to take an extra vehicle."

For some ridiculous reason, Evan felt his face turn a shade darker. "Thanks, brother, but I'm going to be leaving in just a few minutes to pick up a date."

Clancy reared back with surprise. "You're taking an honest-to-goodness date to our sister's Christmas party?"

Evan grimaced. "Why do you sound so shocked? I'm not ready for the retirement rocker yet."

"You'd better not be, because I'm a year older than you," Clancy retorted teasingly. "So who's the woman? Anybody we know?"

"Noelle Barnes. I thought I told you she went with me a couple of weeks ago to visit Granddad and Grandmother. Or maybe I didn't. A lot has happened since then. Work has been crazy."

"The area around here must have had a sudden rash of crimes. You've been away from the house for the past several nights."

Clancy followed his remark with a knowing chuckle, but Evan didn't so much as crack a smile. Now that he'd gotten so much closer to Noelle, he was also beginning to worry himself silly over her safety. And perhaps that was a natural thing, for a man to want to protect the woman he cared for. But he'd never felt this way toward Bianca, and for a while she'd been his fiancée. Did that mean he was already in love with Noelle?

"Actually, there are some things going on." Rising to his feet, he stuffed the tails of his shirt into the waistband of his jeans. "And it's worrying me about Noelle. She lives alone, in the middle of nowhere. The body that was found a few weeks ago had been dumped very close to her property. We haven't solved the case yet. I'm afraid she might see something that could put her in danger or be in the wrong place at the wrong time."

Clancy's expression turned to one of concern. "Wow, Evan, you sound serious about this—about her. Are you?"

For the past several days, Evan had been asking himself that very question. Did he want Noelle always to be in his life? Did he want to make a future, a family with her? They hadn't known each other very long. They were still learning about each other. Yet from the moment he'd woken up in the gulch that day and looked into her velvety brown eyes, something had snared his heart. But he'd been so wrong about Bianca that he wasn't sure he could trust his judgment where women were concerned. Maybe there were things about Noelle that he needed to see, but the attraction he felt for her was blinding him.

"I don't know, Clancy. She's nothing like Bianca. In fact, she's the furthest thing from Bianca that you can imagine. And I'll admit I'm crazy about her. Just being with her makes me happy. But as for marriage—well, I don't want one of these disposable relationships that couples seem to have nowadays. Whenever I marry, it's going to be for the rest of my life. I want to make sure I'm getting it right."

With an understanding smile, Clancy reached over and squeezed Evan's shoulder. "Well, just try not to take ten years to figure it out like I did. That's too much time to waste."

Sassy and her husband, Jett, lived on the J Bar S, a nice-size ranch located in the northeast corner of the county and a few miles off the highway that led to Virginia City. During the drive from Noelle's house, Evan explained that Jett had worked as the Calhoun family lawyer for years before they discovered their long-lost half sister. Jett had fallen for Sassy as he helped her figure out the truth about her parentage. And with Jett virtually growing up with the five brothers, he was more to the family than simply a brother-in-law.

"So how long have Jett and Sassy been married?" Noelle asked.

"I can't remember exactly. Probably a little more than two years, and they've been as happy as a pair of songbirds ever since."

She glanced curiously over at him. "You sound as though you're surprised about that."

Evan shrugged. "I guess it does surprise me, in a way. Jett had gone through a hellish marriage and divorce, and Sassy is still very young—much younger than Jett. On top of that, when Jett first met her, she was pregnant. So it wasn't like they had a smooth start. But now—well, she's expecting their second child soon, and I'm happy to say they fit together like a pair of old gloves."

"That's so nice to hear. I'm looking forward to meeting them. But I can't help wondering if I look okay." She cast an anxious glance down at herself. "It's been years since I've gone to a party, and you didn't tell me whether this was going to be a casual or dress-up affair. If we walk into your sister's home and the women are wearing long gowns, I'm going to feel like an idiot."

From behind the steering wheel of his truck, Evan glanced over at Noelle's lovely image. She wore a red dress that draped across her breasts and accentuated her slender waist. A pair of brown knee-high dress boots covered her long legs. Her waist-length hair was twisted into an elaborate knot at the back of her head and secured with a glittery barrette. She looked nothing like the cowgirl who'd shoved him into Lonesome's saddle and guided him out of the dry gulch.

"If you looked any better, I couldn't stand it. Besides, you're worrying for nothing. This is just a family gathering. And Sassy and Olivia are both outdoor girls like you. They surely won't be wearing designer duds. Neither will Rafe's wife, Lilly. She's very down-to-earth, too."

"That's good, because I don't own any designer clothes. Not anymore," she added.

He chuckled. "Come to think of it, I don't own any, either."

She said, "My parents used to have so many social gatherings that I became numb to them. Now the majority of my conversations are with cattle and horses. I hope I can remember how to interact with people. The last thing I want to do is embarrass you in front of your family."

Evan reached across the seat and squeezed her hand. "You could never do that, pretty lady."

She smiled at him, then glanced out the window at the dark landscape. "I hope your family doesn't read too much into my being at the party tonight. That could be embarrassing, too."

"Why?"

Shrugging, she looked over at him. "Because we're lovers. We're not engaged or anything close to it."

"Would you like for us to be? Engaged, that is?"

Her lips parted with surprise, and then she laughed. "Oh, Evan, don't start teasing me with something like that now. I'm already a nervous wreck. Besides, even if you were serious, neither one of us is the marrying kind. So let's just hope none of your family brings up the subject."

Later that night, after Noelle had met Evan's beautiful family and everyone was sitting around the dinner table, her thoughts kept going back to the remark he'd made on the trip over.

Would you like for us to be? Engaged, that is?

Where had that come from? It was true that their relationship had developed rapidly and had grown even deeper since she'd talked to him about Andy and the bitterness she'd carried around for so long. The fact that he'd understood so completely, that he'd been so gentle and consoling, had filled her heart with an ease she'd never expected to feel again.

He was teasing, Noelle. You don't need to start dreaming and wondering whether Evan has marriage on his mind. And even if he did, it would never work. He lives in a mansion with a family who adores him. He isn't going to give that up for a tiny home surrounded with little more than sagebrush and a few crossbred cows.

Trying not to dwell on that somber thought, Noelle turned her attention to the women sitting around the table. Sassy was heavy with child, and Olivia's pregnancy was beginning to show. Along with those two, Lilly and Rafe had just made the surprise announcement a few minutes ago that they were expecting a second child. Babies were blooming in the Calhoun family, and Noelle couldn't help but look at the women with a bit of envy.

Even though she'd come from a dysfunctional family and she'd learned nothing about mothering from Maxine Barnes, Noelle had always longed to have children of her own. Because she'd seen all the mistakes her parents had made with her and Andy, she'd believed she could be a good and loving parent. After her divorce, she hadn't allowed herself to think much about babies or the fact that she might miss out on being a mother altogether. But seeing the Calhoun women pregnant was a stark reminder that the chance to have a baby of her own was steadily slipping away.

"If I thought a woman like Noelle would rescue me, I'd go out and deliberately fall off Gunsmoke."

Finn's remark broke into Noelle's thoughts, and she looked down the table to Evan's redheaded brother. So far this evening, she could see that Finn was the jokester of the bunch, and his wide smile was infectious.

"You'd never be so lucky," Orin, the brothers' father, spoke up with a teasing grin. "The buzzards would probably find you first."

Next to her, Evan looked at her and smiled. "If Noelle hadn't shown up when she had, the buzzards would have been after me. Or a coyote looking for an easy meal."

At the end of the table, Bart Calhoun, the patriarch of the family, peered at her with a pair of hooded blue eyes. Evan had told her that his grandfather was eighty-four and had suffered a stroke two years ago. But to look at him, she would've never guessed his age, much less that he'd ever had a serious medical problem. He was a robust, authoritative figure of a man.

"We all thank you, Noelle, for taking care of Evan," he said. "You're a brave lady. Nine out of ten women would've galloped off and let someone else deal with getting him back to safety."

Noelle was about to tell Bart that he was giving her too much credit when Evan spoke up in a joking voice, "If I remember right, she told me she'd do as much for an injured dog. So she made me feel rather special."

"Oh, Evan, that's awful," Noelle scolded him. "Your family is going to think I'm a mean person."

Everyone laughed at that, and beneath the table, Evan reached over and squeezed her knee. She slanted him a look, and the glint in his eyes did more than warm her. It made her feel like a part of him and part of his family.

"Far from it, Noelle." Jett joined in the conversation. "We all happen to think that Evan has finally met his match."

Noelle didn't know what to say to that, but Sassy saved her from the awkward silence by grabbing her husband's arm and giving it an affectionate shake.

"Jett! You're embarrassing Noelle! You don't need to be pestering her with that kind of talk!"

"Okay," he relented and looked over at his pretty wife. "We'll talk about Bella's house plans. She's going to move out on us. Two kids in the house is going to be too much for her."

The dark-haired woman, who'd been introduced to Noelle as Jett's sister, let out a good-natured groan. "You *are* being a rascal tonight, Jett. It has nothing to do with the babies. I just feel like it's time for me to have a house of my own and give you and Sassy some privacy. And I've picked out the most beautiful place here on the ranch to build it."

"The only problem with it is that she's going to be a hoop and a holler from Noah's line shack, and he doesn't like neighbors."

Bella made a face as she forked a piece of food on her plate. "That ranch foreman of yours will just need to get used to having a neighbor, because that little pine grove on the hill is going to be my home."

For the next few minutes, Bella talked about her dream house. Then the conversation turned to other things. Eventually, the meal ended and everyone migrated to the living room, where a roaring fire was blazing in the fireplace. In front of a wide picture window, a huge fir tree twinkled with hundreds of lights and glittering ornaments. So many gifts had been stacked beneath the branches that the brightly wrapped boxes had spilled onto the floor several feet out from the tree.

Noelle and Evan took a seat close together on the couch. As she looked around the room, she could think only how she'd been in all sorts of fancy houses, attending elaborate parties, but none of them had looked or felt this warm or beautiful to her. She was surrounded by a family who loved each other, who stuck together through good and bad. To be a part of them, even for one brief evening, was a true Christmas gift to her. One that she would always treasure.

Much later that night, as they walked into Noelle's house, Evan said, "I hope you enjoyed the party. My family can be a little overbearing at times with all their teasing. But they do it only to people they like. And they liked you, Elle."

Smiling, she unbuttoned her coat. "And I liked all of them. I had a lovely time, Evan. I feel bad because I didn't take a present, though. You didn't tell me they were going to pass gifts around."

Evan reached to help ease the coat off her shoulders. "I didn't know they were planning that," he told her. "Sassy said not to bring a thing. So you shouldn't feel bad. She and Jett wanted to do that for all of us. They were just simple little presents anyway. I got a penlight. What was your gift? I forgot."

"It's in my purse. A day calendar with pictures of horses on each page. I love it."

He tossed her coat along with his onto a nearby chair, then wasted no time in pulling her into his arms. "And I loved having you there with me," he whispered as he rested his forehead against hers. "You've made everything more special for me this Christmas."

A breathless laugh passed her lips. "It's not Christmas yet, Evan. We still have a few days to go."

Growling with need, he shifted her in his arms until the juncture of her hips was aligned with his. "It feels like Christmas to me. And it's certainly not too early to start celebrating your birthday, don't you think?"

With another soft laugh, she brought her lips against

his. "I'm in a festive mood, and you're making me feel very special," she said in a low, seductive tone. "Maybe we do need to keep the party going."

Bending, he picked her up and started toward the bedroom. "That's just the answer I wanted to hear."

For the next four days, Evan was swamped with work. The more he and Vincent dug into the evidence they'd gathered on the Watson case, the more both men were leaning toward the homicide being connected to the cattle rustling that had plagued neighboring Douglas County in the past few months. Had Watson known the rustlers and threatened to squeal to the authorities? He'd been a truck driver. Maybe he'd supplied the transportation for moving the cattle and had decided he wanted more money for his part in the thefts? Evan's captain called their theory little more than supposition. He wanted proof, and Evan was determined to give it to him.

"Well, that didn't help a damned bit," Vincent muttered as he punched End on his cell phone. "The Douglas County deputy I just spoke to said they were overloaded with other cases and didn't know when they would get around to questioning the slaughterhouses in their area."

From his seat behind the steering wheel, Evan glanced over at his partner. So far today, the two of them had spent hours driving from one side of the county to the other, interviewing anyone and everyone who'd had even a remote connection to the victim. The day was already getting late, and Evan still wanted to show Vincent the cave area located near the gulch where he'd fallen from Lonesome.

"No need to fret over it," Evan said. "I figure the

rustlers hauled the cattle far away from here. Probably even out of state."

"Why take a chance on going across state lines and getting caught at a highway weigh station?" Vincent tossed the question at him. "That doesn't make sense. Turning them into steak removes the evidence."

"That's true. But you're thinking smart. Most criminals are dumb. You know that. These thugs might have a buyer somewhere who's willing to pay top dollar. And the way the cattle market is right now, anything with hooves and horns brings a chunk of money."

"Well, it sure would be a help if we could find Billy Stivers. But he seems to have gone AWOL. And the poor old aunt we just talked to for a second time— she's clueless."

Evan pushed out a heavy breath. "Yeah, unfortunately, in her mind Billy is just a nice boy who's had some tough breaks."

As the truck rounded another bald hill, the land opened up to a wider vista. Off to the left, Noelle's little house and barn came into view. Before he'd met her, Evan would've driven by the modest homestead and never given it a second glance. Now whenever he saw it, he was filled with an incredible sense of homecoming. Because Noelle was there.

"So who lives over there? Have you talked to those people?" Vincent asked.

Since Vincent had been busy the day Evan worked the crime scene where Watson's body was discovered, his partner wasn't yet familiar with the area.

"You could say so. That's where Noelle lives," Evan said.

Vincent's jaw dropped as he stared at Evan. "There?

That's where the woman lives who's turned you into a dreamy-eyed sap? I don't believe it!"

Trying not to let Vincent's remark offend him, he eased his foot off the accelerator and searched the barnyard for a chance view of Noelle. By now he'd learned her daily schedule. She'd probably already headed out to the pasture with a load of feed and hay for the cattle.

Since the day they'd argued about him hiring someone to build fence for her, he'd managed to drive out early enough to help her with the feeding for a couple of evenings. He'd wanted to make a point of showing her that he was sincere about helping her. As a result, he'd been surprised at how much he'd enjoyed the chores. He wished he had the time to help her more.

"Why?" Evan asked curtly. "Noelle is very proud and devoted to her ranch."

Vincent spluttered. "Why? You live on the Silver Horn. Do I need to say more?"

A spurt of anger tightened Evan's jaw. Just as quickly, it was gone. Vincent's sarcastic reaction made him wonder if that was how Noelle actually viewed him. As someone too lofty ever to have truly serious intentions toward her.

Even if you were serious, neither one of us is the marrying kind.

For the past few days, since Sassy's Christmas party, Noelle's words had lingered in his thoughts and pushed him to examine the feelings steadily growing inside him. He wanted Noelle in his life for more than just a few weeks or months. He wanted her with him for a lifetime. If that meant marriage, then he was going to show her both of them were the marrying kind. And then what? he wondered. He'd be a fool to think she might be willing to make her home on the Silver Horn.

She wasn't about money or luxury. Still, if he could somehow convince her that he loved her and wanted to give her all the things she didn't have now—things that would make her life easier, even safer—then she might view the situation differently.

"Look, Vince, Noelle has already given away more money than you'll probably ever see in your lifetime. That isn't important to her. And it isn't important to me. Maybe it's hard for you to understand. I'll admit that at first, it was hard even for me to fathom. But if you ever come to know her, you'll get it."

"Does that mean you'd be willing to move away from your family and the Horn and make your life here on this isolated, run-down ranch? That would be giving up a hell of a lot, Evan."

Could he do that and still be happy? His father and grandfather expected him to stay on the Horn, even if, or when, he took a wife. They'd be highly disappointed if he moved away.

He let out a heavy breath. "I don't know, Vince. It wouldn't bother me to move into a house that's hardly bigger than the Calhoun family room—"

"You could always build her a new house," Vincent suggested.

Evan let out a short laugh. "She won't even let me hire someone to build fence, much less a new house. Besides, Noelle's little house isn't an issue. It's disappointing my family that concerns me. And in the end, I want to make Noelle's life better. Us living on the Horn would do that and keep my family happy, too."

"But if she's not into money and luxury like you say, she might not go for that idea," Vincent pointed out.

Evan grimaced. "Yeah. That's what worries me. This ranch is her life. And I'm not yet sure where I fit in."

Vincent didn't reply. Instead, he simply looked at Evan as though he was seeing a different man behind the steering wheel. And perhaps his buddy was right, Evan thought as he pressed down on the accelerator to push the truck on past the sight of the ranch yard. Having Noelle in his life was changing him. But was he changing into a better man or just opening himself to another heartache?

A few minutes later, the two men left the truck on the side of the road and walked the few hundred feet to the rock formation Noelle had told him teenagers used as a gathering place. Since the land wasn't fenced and was considered open range, anyone could drive to the spot, so neither man was surprised to see tire tracks leading through the sagebrush and scrubby juniper bushes. But when they followed the tracks to the back of the naturally formed shelter, they found far more than tire tread marks.

"Well, well, what do we have here?" Vincent voiced the question out loud. "Looks like someone has been busy."

A cold chill ran down Evan's spine as he inspected the indentions of cattle hooves and the scrapes along the ground where a portable pen had been erected.

Spotting something yellow among the clumps of dry Indian ricegrass, Evan squatted for a closer look. "We've hit pay dirt, buddy. Here's an ear tag. I doubt it will have any fingerprints on it, but we can hope."

"At least there's a chance that we can trace it back to the rightful owner and go from there."

"I doubt it, but we'll give it a try." Vincent was unfamiliar with all the methods ranches used to identify their livestock, so Evan explained, "Most of those ear numbers are for a rancher's own use to tell one cow from another. Years back, metal ear tags were sometimes used, and they supplied a bit more information. But even those could be cut from the animal's ear. A registered brand burned into a cow's hide is the best proof of ownership."

The two men carefully bagged the evidence, then looked around for more. All in all, they found five more ear tags, two cigarette butts and a small scrap of paper with the partial digits of a phone number.

"Damn. Not enough there to go on," Vincent said. "But everything put together is like finding a gold mine."

"Yeah." Lifting his head from his search of the ground, Evan stared thoughtfully back to the south and Noelle's adjoining land. "The gulch where I fell is just over that rise. As the crow flies, we're not far from Noelle's house."

"Two, two and a half miles at the most," Vincent agreed. "Why? You worried they might strike her place? Steal her horses or cattle?"

"Hell, yes, I'm worried. We don't know what these creeps might do. One man has already been killed. What would they do to a woman alone?"

"Wait a minute, Evan. We don't know for certain that Watson's death is connected to these moonlighters."

Evan muttered a curse under his breath. "Who are you trying to kid?"

"Okay. I'm trying to reassure you, because I can see you're extremely troubled by this."

"This and a lot of things," Evan muttered.

Vincent took off his cowboy hat and swiped a hand through his dark hair. "Evan, back there when we passed Noelle's place…I didn't mean to insult you or her. Hell, I'm not a snob and neither are you." He slapped his hat back on his head. "And now that you've explained what kind of woman she really is, I'm thinking maybe you ought to marry her, Evan. And convince her to leave this place. That would fix all your worries."

"That's just it, Vince, I'm not sure she'd give up this place for me or anybody. She's independent and stubborn. And determined to prove herself."

"To you?"

Evan let out a heavy breath. "To everyone."

Chapter Eleven

A day later, on Christmas Eve, Noelle took care of her outside chores, then returned to the house and baked herself an Italian cream cake for her birthday. Usually she didn't do anything to acknowledge that she'd turned a year older. But Evan had been insisting that she treat herself on her birthday. And eating a slice of decadent dessert would definitely be a treat. Especially if Evan showed up this evening to eat with her, she thought hopefully.

Yesterday afternoon, he'd called to tell her something unexpected had developed with the Watson case and he wouldn't be able to join her that night. During their brief conversation, he hadn't mentioned her birthday or whether he would try to see her. And Noelle hadn't asked. She'd never been the pushy sort, and she realized his demanding job left him with a lot on his mind. For all she knew, he might've gotten distracted and forgotten that Christmas Eve was her birthday.

By seven o'clock that evening, without a word or sign of Evan, Noelle had decided that Evan wasn't going to show. She'd delayed eating the special meal she'd prepared of baked ham and accompanying vegetables, thinking she'd rather wait for him to share the dinner with her. But now it was clear that she'd be eating alone.

Well, she shouldn't let that fact disappoint her, she

thought as she sat at the kitchen table and stared at the covered pots she'd left warming on the stovetop. She'd grown used to being alone on her birthday. She'd chosen to live on this isolated ranch, far away from the family and friends she'd had in Phoenix. Yet this year, with Evan entering her life, she'd hoped things would be different. Now she wondered whether she'd been a fool for believing she was becoming important to him.

Hating the tears that were trying to form in her eyes, she wiped them with a napkin, then walked over to the cabinet. It was silly of her to cry, she scolded herself as she pulled down a plate. Evan wasn't her husband. He wasn't even her fiancé. She shouldn't expect him to make a big deal about her birthday. She shouldn't expect anything more than what he'd been giving her. A few special nights spent in his arms. Yet there was a part of her that yearned for more and needed much more.

She was plucking a clean fork from the dish drainer when she heard a knock on the door. Dropping the utensil onto her plate, she hurried to the living room and carefully peeped around the curtain.

Evan was standing on the step!

Her heart suddenly soaring with joy, she jerked open the door.

"Happy birthday, Christmas angel," he greeted her, then stepped across the threshold and planted a long, long kiss on her lips.

Once he finally lifted his head, Noelle looked at his smiling face and very nearly burst into happy tears. "Wow! That was quite a greeting," she murmured. "Especially after I'd given up on seeing you today."

"On your birthday? Not a chance."

He stepped to one side, and she carefully shut the door behind them.

"Well, I hadn't heard from you and—" Her voice trailed away as he pulled a potted Christmas cactus from behind his back. The plant was covered with beautiful red blooms. "Is that for me?"

He handed the plant to her along with a tiny birthday card attached that read: Happy Birthday, Elle. "The rest of your gift is waiting in the truck."

Confused, she looked at him and chuckled. "What does this mean? You got me a new set of tires or something?"

A teasing grin twisted his lips. "I'd be glad to buy you a new set of tires, honey. But this gift is more fun than that. At least, I think so. Get your coat and I'll show you."

"Now? But supper—"

"We'll eat later. I want you to have your gift first."

As far as she was concerned, her gift was him and his company. But seeing he was excited about showing her this mysterious gift, she gave in. "Okay, Detective Calhoun. Whatever you say."

Once she'd fetched her coat and pulled it on, he took her by the arm and led her out of the house. A lamp illuminated the front yard and made it easy to see where he'd parked his black truck.

As he led her toward the vehicle, he said, "I wasn't sure I was going to be able to pull this off today. That's why I'm late."

"I don't understand. If this is a cake, I hate to disappoint you. I've already made myself one. It's going to be our dessert."

He laughed, and the infectious joy in his voice made her even more eager to see what was waiting for her inside the truck.

"It's nothing to eat," he assured her. "So close your eyes and don't open them until I tell you to."

"Oh, Evan, you're making too big a deal out of this," she protested.

"Your birthday is a big deal to me. Now do as I say and close your eyes."

She shot him an impish smile, then obeyed. "Okay, I can't see a thing."

She heard the door unlatch. "All right. You can look now."

Once he'd opened the back door of the club cab, the interior light had come on. Sitting on the backseat was a German shepherd with two matching pups cuddled close to her side. All three animals were thumping their tails and whining as if to say they couldn't get out fast enough to see their new home.

Stunned, Noelle slowly stepped forward. "Dogs," she murmured with amazement. "Where did they come from? Are they supposed to be mine?"

By now she'd reached Evan's side. He slipped his arm around her waist and urged her closer to the open door of the truck.

"They are completely yours. That is, if you want them. I realize dogs are a big responsibility. But I know how you love animals, and you don't have a dog," he said. "And this mother and her babies needed a home."

She looked at him with wry skepticism. A dog of this sort would never have a problem finding a home. Most likely he'd paid a fortune for them. But for once, Noelle didn't care. "Really? I somehow doubt that," she said with a knowing smile.

His grin was sheepish. "Well, I have a friend who trains dogs, and he has too many. He said I'd be doing him a favor to take them off his hands. But he didn't want to separate the babies from their mother. So I told him I knew the perfect lady to give them a nice home where they'd have plenty of space to run and play. And don't worry. They're outside dogs. We can make them a bed in the barn. The mother is very nice and doesn't bite, but she will bark and warn you if anyone comes around, so that will be good. Do you like them?"

Noelle slipped her arms around his waist and tilted her lips up to his. "I love them. Thank you, Evan. The dogs are the nicest birthday gift I've ever received."

He lowered his head until his lips were touching hers. "I'm glad, Elle. I want you to be happy. Always."

The next morning, Christmas arrived with a flurry of snow and a north wind that whipped across the desert hills. Noelle rose early, and after downing a quick cup of coffee, she hurried to the barn to tend to her chores. Last night before he'd left, Evan had invited her to eat Christmas dinner with his family at the Silver Horn. Though he wasn't supposed to pick her up until mid-morning, she wanted to be ready and waiting.

Inside the barn, the dogs were excited to see her. After doling out breakfast to the livestock, she spent a good deal of time feeding and playing with the beautiful shepherds. The trio was going to be a great deal of company to her, but she would keep them penned in the barn for another day to give them time to understand that this was their new home and they were not to run away.

Along with the dogs, Evan had brought an enormous amount of food with appropriate nutrition for the mother and the pups. It would be weeks before she'd need to buy more. She'd been overwhelmed by his gift, and each time she hugged the dogs, her heart nearly burst with emotion.

Noelle had owned only one dog in her life, and that had been as a young teenager. The little dachshund had been her best buddy until he'd dug beneath the yard fence and run into the street. After Jimmy was killed, she was so distraught that her father had forbidden her to have any more pets. As time had moved on, she'd decided that investing love in a pet was only asking for heartache, and she'd had enough of that to last a lifetime. But now the shepherds had already melted her heart, and she realized that Evan had known exactly what she needed.

Eventually she said goodbye to the dogs and hurried back to the house to get ready for Evan's arrival and the day ahead. She was stepping out of the shower and wrapping a towel around herself when she heard a knock on the door and Evan's voice called out to her.

"Noelle? Are you in there?"

Oh, my, what was he doing here this early? she wondered. He wasn't supposed to be here for another hour! "I've just stepped out of the shower. I'll be right there," she called back.

Grabbing her robe, she jerked it over her dripping body and stepped out of the bathroom, only to find him waiting in the hallway.

She squealed with shock and delight as he swept her forward and into the circle of his arms.

"Evan! I'm wet!"

"Merry Christmas, darling!"

The lengthy kiss he planted on her lips was so all-consuming, she was practically panting by the time he lifted his head. "Merry Christmas back to you," she murmured.

"I've always wanted to know what it would feel like to kiss a Christmas angel." His eyes glinting at her, he ran the tip of his tongue over his lips. "It's just as delicious as I dreamed it would be!"

Chuckling, she smacked a quick kiss on his cheek, then gently scolded him, "You're not supposed to be here this early! Now you're going to have to wait for me to get dressed. And I have no intention of hurrying. I want to look extra nice today when we have dinner with your family."

"I have no intention of hurrying you. I want you to forget about dressing for a minute and come out here to the living room with me. I have something to give you."

"A Christmas gift?" she asked as he led her out of the short hallway. "I thought we'd agreed that we weren't going to give each other a Christmas gift. Besides, you've already given me the dogs."

He chuckled wickedly. "I had my fingers crossed behind my back when I made that promise. And the dogs were for your birthday. They don't count."

"The dogs are great. That's why I'm late getting dressed. I've been down at the barn playing with them." With an impish grin, she pulled away from him and crossed over to a small table where a box was wrapped in festive blue-and-green paper and topped with a big silver bow.

When she carried the gift over to him, he looked at her with such comical surprise that she had to laugh. "I confess. When we made that agreement about not buying Christmas gifts, I had my fingers crossed, too." She handed him the box. "Open yours first."

Easing down on the couch, he unwrapped the package. Once the gift was revealed, he began to laugh. "A Wyatt Earp lunch box! I can't believe you remembered me telling you I always wanted one when I was a boy. Where in the world did you find this treasure?"

Feeling happier than she could remember, she sat down beside him. "Oh, I had a little elf help me search. It took us a while to find one, but we managed to get it delivered in time."

"Jessi?"

Noelle shot him a coy look. "I won't divulge my connections. So do you like your gift?"

"I love it. It's going straight to my office."

"With a sandwich and chips in it?" she joked.

He laughed. "No. To sit on my desk so I can show it off."

Leaning over, he placed a tender kiss on her lips, then gently pushed the tendrils of wet hair from her cheek. "Thank you, sweetheart. The gift is very special to me. Now close your eyes and hold out your hand so that I can give you yours."

Feeling as though Santa had truly come to her house, she held out her hand. "Why do I have to close my eyes again? So you can put a lizard or something in my palm?"

He feigned a hurt look. "Rafe and Finn are the pranksters. Not me. And would I do something like that on Christmas morning?"

She squeezed her eyes tight. "Okay. I'll close my eyes, but this better not be something scary or you're going to be in trouble," she warned him.

"I don't know if you'll think it's scary or not."

The sudden tenderness in his voice should have alerted her to expect a surprise, especially after last night's gift, but nothing could have prepared her for the shock she felt when she opened her eyes and found herself staring at an open ring box and a ring that looked suspiciously like an engagement ring.

Dazed, she touched her fingertip to the large, square-cut stone flanked by sapphires and fashioned in an antique setting. The ring was lovely without being ostentatious. But what did it mean?

"I don't understand, Evan." She shook her head. "This is— It doesn't make sense! This is my Christmas gift?"

His green eyes were full of soft, gentle emotions that she'd never seen before, and her heart began to pound at an incredible pace.

"Yes, your Christmas gift today—and for the rest of your life. I realize we haven't been together that long. And we've not talked about anything like this. But I think you already know how I feel about you."

"Do I?" she asked hoarsely.

Scooting closer, he took the ring box and set it aside, then gathered her hands tightly between his. "Oh, Elle, surely you can tell how much I care about you. How important you've become to me. I love you. And I would be honored and very, very happy if you'd marry me."

Stunned, Noelle stared at him as rays of joy and hope begged her to open her heart and accept his love. Yet at the same time, doubts and questions rained down, muddling her ability to think much of anything.

"I don't know what to say," she finally murmured.

"It's not a confusing question, Elle. All you need to do is say yes." Cupping his hand beneath her chin, he studied her torn expression. "Unless you don't want to spend the rest of your life with me. Is that what you're thinking?"

A bewildered groan tore from her throat. "I care very much for you, Evan. To be honest, I think I fell in love with you the very first day we met. That's why I was so awful to you—because I didn't want to feel the things you were making me feel. Everything about you was scaring me and reminding me I was still a woman, something that I'd let myself forget."

Hope brightened his eyes and spread his lips into a smile. "I think I fell in love with you that day, too. And now—we have our whole lives ahead of us to be together. I'm going to give you everything you need or want. Once we make our home on the Horn, you won't have to lift a finger. You won't have to get out in the bitter cold to feed cows. You won't have to dig postholes, ride fence lines or worry about a calf being stillborn." Lifting her palm to his lips, he kissed the callused skin just below the juncture of her fingers. "I want to make you happy, Elle."

The moment she'd heard him say he loved her, she was certain she'd felt a piece of heaven settle in her heart. But all of that amazing happiness had been wiped away with the words he'd just spoken.

Easing away from him, she rose to her feet. If she hadn't been sopping wet and wearing nothing but a robe, she would've dashed out the door and kept running until she was far out on the range, away from this man who was twisting her heart into a painful knot.

"I'm sorry, Evan," she said stiffly, "but that isn't going to happen."

Jumping up, he caught her by the arm and turned her so she was facing him. "I don't understand, Noelle."

Pain and disappointment plunged through her. "That's why I can't accept your engagement ring—I can't marry you. Because you don't understand," she said.

"Then tell me why! Make me understand this. Because right now my head is spinning. You just said you loved me. Isn't that enough? Isn't that all we need to pledge our lives to each other? The rest will follow."

She pressed her lips tightly together as she tried to gather her splintering senses. "No. What would follow is the way you want things to be, Evan. Not the way I ever hoped or dreamed they would be." Shaking her head, she shoved the wet hair back from her face and tried to brace her heart against the pain rushing through her like a dark tidal wave. "I think you'd better go. This isn't going to work. Not now. Not ever."

"I'm not leaving," he said forcefully. "Not until you explain yourself."

The fact that he seemed clueless to her needs and wants was enough to shove away her pain and replace it with outright anger.

"I guess being a Calhoun makes you think everyone envies your lifestyle—your wealth. I thought you knew me better. I thought you understood how much this land—my home—means to me." With palms up, she thrust her hands at him. "I don't resent my calluses, Evan. I wear them with pride. They mean I'm doing something worthwhile. I'm doing something that gives me deep-down happiness. This land, this house will always be my home. When I had nothing to live for, the ranch gave me purpose and meaning. Without it, I'd be lost."

"And what about me? You wouldn't be lost without me?"

"Oh, yes, it will hurt not having you here with me. But on the other hand, I can see you'd be miserable here. We…we're not the same type of people. For a while, I'd hoped we were. I'd hoped that someday you'd come around to wanting to make your life here with me. Now I can see I was wrong. My home is simple. I'll admit it's even a bit shabby. But I'm proud of it, and I'd be proud if you'd make it your home, too. Yet I can see it's not nearly good enough for you. If I ever do marry, Evan, it will be to a man who wants to be just as self-reliant as I am."

Anger suddenly sparked in his eyes, and his jaw grew so tight she wondered what kept his molar teeth from breaking beneath the pressure.

"And what is that supposed to mean?" he asked. "I'm not living off dividends from the ranch. I told you that!"

"You continue to live on the Silver Horn to appease your dad and grandfather. Because you feel guilty. Because you think that makes up somehow for turning your back on ranching and becoming a lawman."

"You're right," he admitted. "I would feel guilty. My grandfather and father have worked hard to give me and my brothers a wonderful home. And they've done it honestly and with love. I'm asking you to make it your home, too. Can't you see I want to give things to you? Not take things away."

Shaking her head, she stared hopelessly at the worn linoleum beneath her feet. Her heart ached, and she figured it would go on aching for the rest of her life. "I understand that, Evan," she mumbled. "I can see you want to make things easier for me—to pamper me. But that isn't what *I* want. I gave up that sort of life to come here to Nevada and make something of this ranch and myself. I can't do that if everything is handed to me. And in the end, I wouldn't be happy living in that fancy ranch house at the Silver Horn."

"Not even with me?" he asked, his voice strained and low.

Even though a shaft of pain was stabbing her chest, she forced herself to look at him. "Not even with you."

"If that's how you feel, then I sure as hell don't need to keep hanging around, begging you to become my wife. Because if I ever marry, it's going to be to a woman who cares more about me than she does about a piece of damned dirt and a measly herd of cattle!"

Before she could make any sort of reply to that, he grabbed up his hat and jacket and jerked open the door.

"Merry Christmas, Noelle! You've certainly made this one unforgettable!"

She didn't try to stop him as he stepped outside and slammed the door behind him. What would be the point? Trying to make things work with Evan would be like trying to make hay in the rain. All she'd wind up with was a moldy mess.

Her eyes filling with tears, she turned to leave the room and noticed he'd left the ring box on the couch with the lid still open. As she picked it up, the diamond seemed to wink mockingly at her. Noelle couldn't help remembering all the Christmases in the past when she'd received valuable gems as a gift. She'd spent those holidays alone, too, she thought miserably.

Snapping the lid shut, she placed the box next to the poinsettia he'd given her two weeks ago. To make her little house look more like Christmas, she thought ruefully. He hadn't understood then, any more than he did today, that Christmas had nothing to do with decorations and everything to do with the gift of love.

By the time New Year's Eve rolled around, Noelle had hardened herself to the fact that everything she'd ever hoped to have with Evan was over. Now that her anger at him had cooled, she could view the situation clearly, and it was easy to see that the two of them wanted different things in their lives. Ending their relationship before they got any deeper had been for the best. Still, that didn't make it any easier to bear the ache of loneliness that never seemed to leave her.

What are you thinking, Noelle? How could things get any deeper than loving a man with all your heart? You've never felt anything like this for any man, including your ex-husband. And chances are you'll never feel this much for any man again. So what are you going to do? Do as Evan accused you of doing? Throw it all away for a piece of land and a herd of cows?

Fighting to shove away the mocking voice in her head, she tossed the saddle onto Lonesome's back and cinched the girth. The fact that the Silver Horn horse was still residing in her barn was a mystery to her, and she'd considered calling the ranch to have someone come to collect the animal. But she'd fallen in love with the paint. Though she knew she'd eventually have to give him up, she didn't want to think about that day until she was actually faced with it.

At least she had the dogs. And though they were a joy, each time she watched them at play around the ranch yard, she couldn't help but remember the night Evan had given them to her. On her birthday, he'd made her feel so loved, so special.

A brush against her leg had her looking down to see the mother dog, Gracie, standing at her side and looking up at her with eager anticipation.

"I know you'd like to go, Gracie, but your little ones couldn't keep up. Their legs aren't long enough yet. You need to stay here and watch over them until Lonesome and I get back. Now go on. Go find your babies," she told the dog.

Thankfully, the shepherd did as she was told. Noelle grabbed the reins and urged the horse from beneath the shed of the barn. "Come on, Lonesome, let's ride out and see if the cattle are finding any grass. What do you say?"

The horse gave her shoulder a gentle nudge, and No-elle suddenly found tears in her eyes and a lump in her throat. Turning, she wrapped her arms tightly around his neck and pressed her cheek against his winter coat.

"At least you understand me, boy, even if Evan can't," she told the horse. Then, with a determined sniff, she climbed into the saddle and reined the horse into the bitter north wind.

Ten minutes later, she and Lonesome arrived at the spot where she'd fed the cattle yesterday evening. The hay she'd spread for them had all been eaten, but there was no sign of the cows.

Believing the herd had moved farther north in search of grass, she kicked Lonesome into a long trot and continued to search the jagged horizon for the cattle. But by the time she reached the gulch with no sign of the animals, an uneasy feeling hit her.

It wasn't like the cows to be this far away from the ranch yard. Not at this time of the year, when grazing was scarce and they were accustomed to being fed routinely.

Trying not to panic, Noelle urged Lonesome down the steep bank of the gulch. Once they reached the bottom, she started up the narrow draw, then reined the horse to a stop and stared in shock at the sight in front of her. Hundreds of cattle tracks marred the silt and dirt. Even to her untrained eye, it was easy to determine by the deep tears in the earth that the cattle had been running, not meandering along searching for grass.

Sick to her stomach, Noelle followed the trail until it reached the end of the draw. There the cattle had been pushed up the bank and onto the plateau where she'd finished repairing the boundary fence not too many days ago.

Directing Lonesome up the bank, she prayed with all her might that she would find the cattle there on the flat land and that her fear they'd been stolen was wrong. God willing, the cattle had simply run into the gulch in an effort to get away from coyotes or wolves.

But that hope was squashed flat the moment she and Lonesome topped the steep bank. Part of the fence lay on the ground.

"Oh, dear God." Her livelihood, everything she owned had been poured into that herd. Now they were gone, wiped away as though she'd never had them.

What was she going to do now? Call Evan?

She'd pretty much told Evan she didn't need his kind of help. It wouldn't be right for her to go asking for it now. She'd have to deal with this on her own. The way she'd done everything on her own since she'd decided to change her life and move to Nevada.

Later that day at the sheriff's office, Evan was doing his best to concentrate on the notes scattered over his desk, but thoughts of Noelle, along with Vincent's chatter, kept spoiling his effort to focus on the Watson case.

"You should've come over to my house last night to help me celebrate New Year's Eve," Vincent said. "There was a dandy NBA game on, and I even had pizza delivered. I ate the whole thing by myself. What did you do, anyway?"

"I was here. Working."

Using a foam cup as a basketball, Vincent tossed it into a high arc, then grinned triumphantly as it dropped neatly into a nearby trash basket.

"Hell, man, there's no use in you trying to kill yourself over this case. It'll get solved. You need to give it time to let the pieces fall into place."

"The pieces won't fall into place on their own. They have to be fitted together by someone," Evan barked at him. "And today is New Year's Day. The way I remember our schedule, you didn't have to show up today. So why are you here?"

The other man shrugged. "I didn't have anything better to do. And I figured you needed someone around to cheer you up. Ever since Miss Barnes gave you that big fat no, I've been trying to decide if you need a bottle of whiskey or a night on the town."

Evan slammed his pencil onto his desk. "Damn it, Vince, I don't find that funny. I don't find you funny. Why the hell don't you just go home and leave me alone?"

Unaffected by his partner's outburst, Vincent walked over to Evan's desk and picked up the Wyatt Earp lunch box sitting next to a banker's lamp. "You know what? I don't find you a bit amusing, either. In fact, you're coming across to me as damned pathetic."

Evan started to blast him with another angry retort, then caught himself as he realized he was behaving like a jackass. And it was hardly fair to take his misery out on his partner.

"Sorry, Vince. I didn't mean that. I was just sitting here wondering what I'm doing working as a detective. Clearly, I'm in the wrong department."

"Why do you say that?"

"Because I'm supposed to be smart enough to evaluate a situation. To read people. But I got it all wrong with Bianca. It took me far too long to figure out what she was all about. And now with Noelle...well, I've misjudged everything about her. I'm beginning to doubt my judgment on anything anymore."

Vincent shook his head. "You're being too hard on yourself, Evan. Trying to figure out a woman you love is far different than looking analytically at a crime scene. No matter how hard we try, women will always be a mystery to us men. Just when you think you understand what she wants or needs, you learn you've got it all wrong. You're a damned good detective. You can't let this break with Noelle shake your confidence."

Evan sighed. "I know you're right. But I feel like a damned fool. I'll admit I'm not handling this thing with Noelle very well. But I—well, I've never felt like this about any woman before. When she turned me down, I—"

"You were shocked," the other man finished for him. "You didn't expect her to hand that ring right back to you, did you?"

He grimaced. "That ring," he muttered crossly. "I have no idea what she's even done with that ring. Probably crushed it with a sledgehammer. She's not impressed with shiny or showy."

"Then why did you try to give her something shiny and showy? Why didn't you pick out a sweet, simple solitaire? One that didn't shout, 'I'm a Calhoun! I can buy you anything you want'?"

"Do you think that would've made a difference?"

Placing the tin lunch box back on the desk, Vincent regarded him thoughtfully. "It couldn't have hurt."

Shaking his head, Evan leaned back in the office chair and raked both hands through his hair. He'd never felt so tired and defeated in his life. Nor had he ever been so confused or torn. What had started out to be the most beautiful, wonderful Christmas he could imagine had turned into one of the darkest days of his life.

"Offering her a more modest ring won't help, Vince. She wants no part of living on the Silver Horn." Evan sighed. "And I guess, deep down, I knew that she wouldn't. But damn it, I'm not trying to make her change. I just want to make her life better—easier. Isn't that what every man wants to do for the woman he loves?"

"Yeah, I guess it's our nature to want to provide for our mate. But I think we make the mistake of focusing on the wrong thing. I did. Instead of giving Tanya what would make her happy, I tried to give her what I thought she needed. It's no wonder she wanted to blot everything out with alcohol."

Evan had never heard Vincent talk this way. Oh, he'd talked about his ex being an alcoholic before, but just hearing his partner admit to making mistakes with the woman made Evan feel less alone.

"Give her what makes her happy," Evan said. "Yeah. I guess that makes sense. But that means I'd have to quit living with my family and leave the Silver Horn. It means I'd be making my home in that little stucco of hers. It hardly has enough room in it to cuss a cat."

Grinning now, Vincent started back to his desk. "Think about it, Evan. Wouldn't it be better to be in Noelle's warm, loving arms than on the Horn in a big, lonely bedroom?"

My home is simple. I'll admit it's even a bit shabby. But I'm proud of it, and I'd be proud if you'd make it your home, too. Yet I can see it's not nearly good enough for you.

For the past week, Noelle's words had haunted him. She believed he considered himself too good to live in her house. But that simply wasn't true. He'd be happy to live with Noelle in a tent, if necessary. But she wasn't willing to do the same. That was what cut him the deepest. Yet he doubted she would understand his feelings, even if he tried to explain them to her. Maybe he was expecting her to give up too much. Maybe he should've made it clear that he would meet her in the middle. That no matter what, they could work it out.

Evan's troubled thoughts were interrupted when the phone on his desk rang. The extension button for the dispatcher was blinking. He picked up the receiver and said, "Happy New Year, Mia. What's up?"

"Happy New Year to you, too, Evan. And I'm not sure—but I think the call I got a few minutes ago might interest you. It came from a woman out on Black Burro Road. Isn't that where the homicide victim was found?"

Scooting to the edge of his seat, Evan gripped the phone. "What woman? What's happened?"

"Just a second. Uh…here it is. Her name is Noelle Barnes. She called to report her cattle are missing."

A sick sensation hit the pit of his stomach like a shovel full of heavy rocks. Some bastard had taken away Noelle's whole source of income. Even worse, those cattle were like babies to her. Many of them she had named, and she recognized each one on sight. She must be feeling as if the whole world had been ripped from under her feet.

"When?" Evan shot the question at the dispatcher.

"I told you, she called a few minutes ago."

"No! I mean when did the cattle go missing?"

By now Vincent was standing in front of Evan's desk.

"She discovered them gone this afternoon. That's all I know. I assured her someone would be out to investigate. Roberts and Williams are on their way there now."

"Okay, Mia. Thanks."

Leaping to his feet, he tossed the receiver back on its hook. "Noelle's cattle have been stolen! I've got to do something!"

Vincent grabbed for his hat and jacket at the same time Evan reached for his.

"I'll go with you," Vincent said. "With a little luck, the trail might still be hot enough that we can get them back for her."

"It's going to take a whole lot more than luck," Evan said as the two men left the room at a trot.

Chapter Twelve

Blinking at the moisture building in her eyes, Noelle plunged her hands into the dishwater. She refused to cry. Tears wouldn't bring her cattle back. She'd cried a bucket of tears over Evan, and they certainly hadn't brought him back to her.

She was scrubbing fiercely at a spot of dried food on the rim of a saucepan when a knock sounded on the doorjamb behind her.

Whirling around in fright, she stood with her hands dripping and stared at Evan standing just inside the kitchen.

"I didn't hear Gracie bark. What are you doing here?" she asked bluntly.

He stepped forward until he was standing in the middle of the room. As his eyes met hers, Noelle thought her heart would surely split with longing and pain. Had it been only a week since he'd walked out the door? It felt as if months of gray, dreary days had passed since she'd touched him, kissed him, felt his strong arms holding her close.

"I'm here about the cattle," he said.

"I've already told the deputies everything I know."

"Vincent and I will be the investigators on this case. The deputies were just here to take the initial report of what happened."

Turning her back to him, she reached for a dish towel to dry her hands. "Well, send Vincent in, then," she said stiffly. "I'd rather talk with him."

Crossing the short distance between them, he stood a few inches down the counter from her. "I'm the one in charge of this interview, Noelle. Not you. And not Vince."

"Well, bully for you. I'm missing my cattle, and you're more worried about who's in charge of the situation." She glared at him. Mostly because being angry with him was so much easier than dwelling on how much she loved him. "I don't give a damn if you're in charge or the governor of this state! All I care about is getting my herd back! Got it?"

His nostrils flared as he studied her for long, silent moments. "Yeah, I got it. You can play the tough girl all you want with me. But I understand how much you're hurting over this. I wanted to talk to you tonight because I thought it would make you feel better to learn I'd be working this case. That I'm making a promise to you now to get your cattle back. But I guess that means nothing to you. I mean nothing to you."

His last words caused tears to blur her eyes and her throat to tighten to the point that she could scarcely breathe. Desperate to hide her broken emotions, she turned her back to him and swiped at her eyes with the back of her hand.

"The more you talk, the worse it gets," she mumbled. "All that time we spent together—you didn't hear anything I said, except what you wanted to hear."

Suddenly his hands were wrapping around her upper arms, while the front of his body was pressing into her back. "If I'm supposed to understand any of that, I'm sorry. You're going to have to be plainer with me."

Bending her head, she struggled to stop herself from turning and flinging herself against his chest and seeking the comfort of his strong arms.

"Just because I'm angry with you doesn't mean I've stopped loving you, Evan," she said hoarsely.

The room became unbearably quiet for long seconds before his cheek pressed against her hair and his lips hovered close to her ear. "Then why are you putting us through this misery? We could be so happy—"

Before he could finish, she whirled out of his arms and lifted her chin defiantly. She faced him head-on. "If I gave up everything and did things your way? No. That wouldn't make me happy, Evan. Even if I tried it, I'd end up resenting you. And I don't want that to happen."

"You wouldn't have to give up this place entirely. I could hire some hands to keep it going."

Frustration had her groaning and shaking her head. "Do you hear yourself? Hire, hire, hire. That's all you think about. Paying someone to do the work that I want to do. I want to keep this place going, Evan. I want to pitch the hay, spread the feed, work the cattle. I want to birth the calves and ride the fences. My herd is gone, but this is still my home. My land. I'll recover somehow. And I'll do it my way."

"Do you hear yourself, Noelle? Instead of meeting me halfway, you're expecting me to change my whole life."

"Your idea of halfway is me living on the Horn while this place slowly turns into nothing more than a piece of land with a few scrub cows on it."

His jaw clamped tight. "That's a low blow, Noelle."

"Yeah, I guess it is. But right now, I'm feeling pretty low." Grabbing up the dish towel, she wiped her hands a second time, then started out of the room. "I'll be right back."

Seconds later she returned with the ring box and slammed it into his hand. "Here's your ring. You might as well take it back, because it doesn't fit."

Scowling now, he looked down at the velvet box. "How do you know? Did you try it on?"

"Size has nothing to do with the fit, Evan."

He started to say something else, but a male voice was suddenly calling to him from the front door.

"Hey, Evan. I've got something. We need to hit the road."

Slipping the ring box into his shirt pocket, he said, "I've got to be going. If we find your cattle, you'll be the first to know."

"Don't worry. I'm not expecting a miracle."

"Lawmen don't deal in miracles. You have to pray for one of those. And you just might ought to do that."

He left the room, and moments later, she heard the front door close behind him. The finality of the sound left a hollow feeling in the middle of her chest and a ball of pain in her throat.

The next morning, Noelle decided she couldn't sit around on her hands and hope things got better. The rustlers had taken her cattle, but they couldn't take her spirit. And neither could Evan.

After dressing in heavy work clothes, she walked down to the barn and saddled Lonesome, then gathered fencing pliers and enough staples to repair the fence at the gulch. She was shoving the equipment into a pair of saddlebags when the dogs began to bark and she heard a vehicle outside the barn.

Leaving the horse tied to a hitching post, she walked

around the cattle pen obstructing her view and was shocked to see Bart Calhoun climbing down from a bright red pickup truck. Even though he was simply dressed in jeans, boots and a brown ranch coat, his broad shoulders and big black cowboy hat made him an authoritative figure of a man.

What was the elder Calhoun doing here? she wondered wildly. Had something happened to Evan, and he'd come to give her the news? The terrifying thought had her jogging out to meet him.

While she called the dogs to her side, he lifted a hand in greeting. "Hello, Noelle. As I passed on the road, I caught a glimpse of you down here at the barn," he explained. "That's why I didn't stop at the house."

"Hello, Mr. Calhoun." She stepped forward and offered him her hand. But rather than shake it, he simply gathered it between his and held on tightly. Noelle was surprised at how much comfort and strength she drew from the connection. Other than the night she'd visited with him at Sassy's party, she didn't really know much about the Calhoun patriarch. Evan had told her that Bart liked to force his will upon the family. But she hadn't seen that side of him yet.

A faint smile touched his weathered face. "I guess you'd like to know what I'm doing here."

"I am surprised to see you," she admitted. "Has something happened to Evan?"

"Not anything you can't fix," he said. Then, putting a hand on her shoulder, he urged her toward the barn. "Let's get out of this wind."

With the dogs trotting at their heels, they walked around the wooden corrals until they reached the side of the barn where Lonesome stood quietly tied to the hitching post. In this spot, the old weathered building shielded them from the north wind, yet the bleak winter sun offered little warmth.

She was still wondering what Bart meant by his remark about Evan when he gestured toward Lonesome. "Were you about to ride out?"

"When the rustlers took my cattle, they cut my fence. I was going out to repair it." She rested a hand on Lonesome's spotted hip. Below it was the C/C brand that marked the Silver Horn livestock. "I suppose you want to know why I have a Silver Horn horse, but no one has ever bothered to come pick him up."

Bart waved a dismissive hand. "Hell, the Horn has too many horses to count. I'm not here about the paint or to plead Evan's case. Whatever happens between you two is your business. I'm here because I heard about your cattle, and I want to help any way I can."

Noelle was stunned. For a man of Bart Calhoun's stature to have a second thought about her predicament, much less drive nearly an hour to see her, was incredible.

"I'm very grateful to you, Mr. Calhoun. It's very, very nice of you to offer, but I'll get through this the best way I can."

"First of all, I want you to call me Bart. And second, you can ask anyone in this county and they'll tell you I'm not necessarily a nice man. If I do anything, it's usually with a selfish motive."

Appreciating his honesty, she slanted him a questioning look. "And what could you possibly gain out of helping me?"

He pointed to her face. "Seeing you smile. That would be enough."

"I don't believe that."

Instead of being insulted by her curt reply, he chuckled. "Evan said you could be tough. I see what he meant."

"Well, I don't want to seem ungrateful, Mr.—uh, Bart. In fact, I'm humbled that you're offering to help. But I—"

"You don't even know what my offer is yet. Maybe you should hear it before you start turning it down."

Jamming her gloved hands into the pockets of her coat, she looked out at the single cow and calf pair she had left on the ranch. And the only reason she had them was that she'd corralled them at the barn three days ago in order to doctor the cow for respiratory distress.

"Okay, I'm listening," she told him.

"I'd like to give you another herd of cows. Black Angus or Hereford. Take your pick. If I remember right, Evan tells me you had a hundred head, give or take a few. I'll have a hundred and fifty shipped here before the day is over. They'll all be up on their vaccinations, healthy and bred to calf in the spring. All I ask from you is that you pay me back with half the calf crop. As for a bull, you'll have to come up with one of those on your own. But I know where you could lease one cheap."

Noelle stammered, "Half! Bart— I— You—you're not making sense to me! That wouldn't begin to pay off the cost of the mama cows. No. There's no way I'd do any such deal like that. It's charity. And I won't accept charity!"

"Why? Think you're too good to accept help?"

Even though the wind was icy, she could feel a wave of heat sting her cheeks. She'd accused Evan of thinking he was too good to live in her little house. She hadn't stopped to consider that he might have the same idea about her. That Noelle believed she was too special to go along with his wishes and move to the Silver Horn.

The notion troubled her. "No. But I like to do for my-self. I don't want to be beholden to anyone."

Expecting Bart to be angry, she was surprised when his blue eyes suddenly glinted with admiration. "Okay. If you feel that half the calf crop wouldn't be a fair re-payment, then you could come over to Silver Horn on certain days of the week and work out the rest. I hear you're a good ranch hand. We can always use more help. I'll talk to Rafe about it. He won't have any qualms about having a woman on the crew."

She could see that he was trying his best to help her. More than that, he was trying to make her feel good about accepting help. It dawned on her that, for what-ever reason, he was treating her like family, a real fam-ily that stuck together through good times and bad. The idea touched her heart in a way that had nothing to do with cows or calves or whether, in the coming months, she'd have enough money to put food on the table. It had everything to do with the fact that this man was offering her unconditional love.

"Well, I'm not going to say yes just yet," she told him. "But I will think about it. In the meantime, maybe Evan will get my cattle back."

"Never hurts to hope, Noelle." He gestured toward the sick cow and its calf. "That's all you have left?"

She nodded. "And the horses."

His gaze turned to the listing barn and the barren vista. Noelle wondered whether he was thinking, like Evan, that she was working herself to the bone for a worthless piece of ground.

"I'm sure this place doesn't look like much to you. But it will someday," Noelle said proudly. "I won't give up."

Turning his attention back to her, he reached over

and gave her shoulder an encouraging pat. "I'd hate like hell if you did." He made a sweeping gesture toward the house and barn and on to the open land beyond. "This might come as a surprise to you, but the Silver Horn hardly amounted to this much when my father started it. A person needs the determination to hold on to a dream, or it won't ever come true."

She swallowed as tears threatened to fill her eyes. "I wish Evan could see things as you do," she said, her voice choked with emotion.

He gave her a gentle smile. "Evan isn't as old or wise as his grandfather. Just give him a little time, Noelle. He'll open his eyes."

She didn't think so. But like Bart had said, she needed to hold on to her dreams. Foolish idea or not, Evan was still a part of them.

She asked, "Would you like to go to the house and have a cup of coffee with me?"

"I can't think of anything I'd like better," he said, "but what about your fence repairs?"

Shrugging, she chuckled. "Oh, that can wait. After all, it's not like the cows are going to get out."

He looked at her and let out a hearty laugh. "Elle, you're my kind of woman. Let's go have that coffee."

Four days later, late Tuesday evening, Evan was dead on his feet, but he refused to follow Vincent's advice to go home and get some much-needed sleep.

"You're still here? You're not going to be able to help Noelle get her cattle back if you wind up in the hospital from exhaustion." Vincent crossed the little office and looked into a paper sack on the edge of Evan's desk.

"You haven't touched the sandwich or anything else in this bag. Have you eaten this evening?"

Without looking up from the scribbled notes in front of him, Evan replied, "I drank a soda. That's all I wanted."

Cursing, Vincent tossed up his hands in a helpless gesture. "Okay, I'll forget about you getting any nourishment or rest. Have you made progress since I've been out this afternoon working the nightclub assault?"

Evan sighed. "No. Each time I think I've latched on to a name that might lead us somewhere, I hit a dead end."

"What about Billy Stivers? Still no luck finding him?"

Rising from the chair, Evan rubbed his fingers against his burning eyelids. "No. I called his aunt again earlier today, but she insists she hasn't heard from him in weeks. From what she tells me, he's been over in California. He wouldn't have any reason to know about Noelle's missing cattle."

Grimacing, Vincent walked over to an armchair pushed against the back wall of the room and practically fell into it. "That might be true. But he's hardly a model citizen. And right now he seems to be our best hope of finding a connection to this crime or even the Watson homicide." He glanced keenly at Evan. "Have you talked with Noelle lately?"

Evan wiped a weary hand over his face. "Not since New Year's Day when we investigated at her place."

Vincent shook his head. "Why? Because you don't want to tell her that her cattle are just as gone now as they were then?"

"No! I just—well, there's just nothing I can say to her."

"Really? Nothing?"

Glaring at him, Evan shuffled to the little table holding the coffee percolator. When he tipped the spout into a foam cup, nothing came out but black, watery dregs. Now Evan would have to wait a good fifteen minutes for another pot to brew. The idea grated on his raw nerves.

"When are we going to get a coffeepot that wasn't made in the 1950s?" he barked at Vincent. "Is it going to take an earthquake to get rid of this antique?"

Vincent jumped from the chair and reached out to snatch the percolator from Evan's grip. "Give me that! I don't want your ungrateful paws on it! I'll make the coffee and—"

Evan held the pot out of Vincent's reach. "I can do it! Leave it—"

"Hey, guys! If you think you can quit fighting over that toy long enough to listen, there's someone here who wants to see you."

At the sound of the deputy's loud voice, both men went stock-still and stared at the open doorway of the office.

"Who?" Evan asked.

"Billy Stivers. I just took him to the interrogation room," the deputy answered.

Shocked by this turn of events, Evan and Vincent swapped hopeful glances.

"What's he been arrested for?" Vincent asked the deputy.

"He's not arrested. I put him in the interrogation room because that was the only empty place I could find. He walked in on his own. Said he'd heard Evan wanted to talk to him, so he decided to come in and find out what was going on."

Evan tossed the coffeepot at his partner and dashed for the door, nearly knocking down the deputy in the process.

"Billy Stivers is going to do some talking. And fast!"

The next afternoon, Noelle happened to be in the house when the phone rang. Hoping and praying it might be Evan with news of her cattle, she made a dive for the receiver.

"Hey, Noelle, it's Jessi."

Noelle's heart sank. "Oh, hi, Jessi."

"Gee, if I'd known my call was going to make you so glum, I would've called earlier."

Jessi's sarcastic reply had Noelle shaking her head. "Sorry, Jessi, if I sound less than enthusiastic. When I heard the phone ring, I was praying it was Evan."

"No doubt. The man holds the key to your happiness."

Noelle let out a weary breath. She didn't want to discuss her broken relationship with Evan. Every cell in her body was exhausted with worry. Every particle of her heart was weighted with sorrow. She didn't want to rehash the pain.

"I'm hoping he'll get my cattle back, Jessi."

"Cattle!" Jessi repeated sardonically. "You can go to the sale barn and buy more of those. You can't replace Evan. Maybe you ought to be pondering that instead of a bunch of bawling cows."

Since Jessi understood very little about livestock or ranching, Noelle could forgive the young woman's ignorance on the importance of her cattle. But on the other hand, Noelle knew her friend had a point. She couldn't replace Evan. Not with anyone or anything.

"Listen, Jessi, not a minute of the day goes by that I don't regret having to give Evan's ring back to him. But he didn't give me any other options."

Jessi let out a long sigh of frustration. "That's because you want everything to be on your terms. From what you told me, he offered to let you keep your ranch. Isn't that enough?"

As Jessi's question rattled around in her head, Noelle swept her gaze over the little living room. Even though her house might be a bit shabby, she'd always loved each and every room. Yet now, without Evan, they all seemed empty and meaningless. Was this the way everything was going to be for her now? she wondered grimly. She'd thought holding on to this place, this dream to build it into a fine ranch, would make her happy. But not without Evan in her life.

Closing her eyes against the pain, she said, "I don't want to talk about it, Jessi. In fact, I have chores down at the barn that I need to be getting to."

"Fine. Hang up because you don't want to deal with the problem. But I have one question you need to consider. What have you been willing to give up for Evan's sake? To meet him halfway?"

The question momentarily stunned Noelle. As her mind began to whirl, reality swept in, leaving her chilled and confused.

Instead of meeting me halfway, you're expecting me to change my whole life.

Evan's words were suddenly knocking at her heart, demanding that she listen. Could Jessi be right? Was Noelle the one who was being selfish and obstinate? Instead of concentrating on all she'd be giving up, perhaps she should be thinking of the things Evan would be giving up by moving to her place. Especially being near his loving family.

"I—I have very little to give up for Evan," she finally said in a choked voice. "My whole life it seems someone has demanded that I give up the things that matter to me most. My morals, my money, my hopes and dreams. My happiness. How much is a woman supposed to keep giving up, Jessi?"

A long silence stretched between the two women. Just when Noelle was about to prod an answer out of her friend, she heard barking dogs and vehicles approaching.

Carrying the phone to the window, she peeped out the curtain and stared in shock at the sight of the trucks and cattle trailers pulling into her drive.

"Jessi! I've got to hang up—"

"Wait just a minute! I'm thinking—"

"Jessi, I have company!" she swiftly interrupted. "It looks like Mr. Calhoun has just driven up with a load of cattle."

Jessi gasped. "You mean Evan? He's found your cattle?"

"No. I mean Bart. I'll call you later."

She jammed the phone back onto its hook, then grabbed her coat and ran out the front door. But after three long strides, she spotted Evan walking toward her. The sight of him caused her to stop dead in her tracks.

"What is this?" she asked when he got within earshot. "I haven't agreed to your grandfather's offer yet."

Pulling up a step away from her, he stood staring at her in confusion. "What are you talking about? What offer?"

At that moment, she figured her expression probably looked far more stunned than his. "To give me the cattle—a hundred and fifty head of pregnant mama cows. All he wants in return is half the calf crop. I'm not sure—"

"Grandfather offered you that? I can't believe it!"

Still uncertain what was going on, she glanced out at the cattle trailers. The bawling cows and calves shifted and stomped for space in the tight confines. Some of them were black and others were brindle brown, just like hers had been. The eldest Calhoun must have thought having the cattle resemble hers would make her feel better.

"Bart didn't come with you?"

Faintly annoyed with her questions, Evan said, "Well, no! Why should he?"

"To finish the deal. And—"

She broke off abruptly as she spotted two men in deputy uniforms climbing out of one of the trucks.

She frowned, perplexed. "What are those deputies doing with you?"

"I couldn't drive both trucks by myself. After I found the cattle, I had to call for help and—"

"Found the cattle!" she burst out. "You mean those are mine? You found my cattle?"

"Yes. Last night. Over in California. They'd just been unloaded at a meat-packing plant."

The relief that rushed through Noelle was so great, it left her weak and swaying on her feet. Leaping forward, Evan grabbed her by the arm to steady her. She fell against his chest and began to weep.

"Oh, Evan. I—don't know what to say. Except that I'm sorry. So sorry."

"Shh. We'll talk about it later," he murmured against

her cheek. "Let me help you to the house so you can sit down."

With his arm tight around her shoulders, he guided her back into the house and over to the couch. Once she was settled and off her feet, he ordered, "Stay right there. Don't move. I'm going to go show the men where to unload the cattle, and then I'll be right back."

While he was gone, she did her best to collect herself, but the moment he walked back through the door, the sight of him caused tears to seep into her eyes.

"Your cows are on their home range, and the deputies are heading to town." Casting her a wry grin, he eased down on the couch beside her. "See? Lawmen are good for a few things."

Still in disbelief, she used her fingers to wipe away her tears. "I can't believe you found the cattle. After all these days, I figured they were either hundreds of miles from here or hanging in a meat-packing refrigerator."

"I'll be honest, Elle, the case was looking pretty bleak until your neighbor's nephew showed up at the sheriff's office."

"Billy Stivers? He's the one who stole them?"

"No. Billy didn't have anything to do with the crime. But because he has ties to some of the local truckers, he had a good idea who might be responsible and his lead actually helped us locate the persons involved." He reached for her hand and drew it onto his lap. "The thieves had branded over the Rafter B on your cattle to turn it into a Diamond B, then hauled them to a small town in California. It's a long story, and I'd rather go into it later. Right now, I want to know what's going to happen to us. I realize that getting your cattle back isn't going to fix our problems. I—"

Before he could say more, she leaned into him and

placed a gentle finger against his lips. "Wait, Evan! I can't let you go on without telling you how wrong and terrible I've been. I was expecting too much of you to move onto this little ranch with me. Especially when you're used to the best of everything. When you love people, you don't want to make them miserable by forcing them to do your will. And that's what I was doing to you. Expecting you to be as proud of this place as I am." Moving her finger away from his lips, she caressed his cheek while marveling at the pleasure of simply touching him again. "I don't know what, if anything, I can do about changing my aunt and uncle's will. It says if I don't live here, it will be sold. But, in the end, if I need to give it up to have you in my life, then I really have no choice. Since we've been apart, I've come to realize that you are more important to me than anything."

He bent his head and covered his face with both hands. Noelle's heart gave a dreadful thud. Did he not believe her? Had she already ruined her chance to have this wonderful man as her husband?

Placing a hand on his shoulder, she asked tentatively, "Evan? Have I said something wrong?"

Another moment of silence passed, and then he lifted his head and gazed into her eyes. "No. You've made me so ashamed that it's hard to look you in the face, my darling. Because I— A moment ago, when you talked about giving up everything you'd ever worked for or wanted, it suddenly dawned on me just how much of a jerk I really am."

"Oh, Evan, that's—"

"No, hear me out, Noelle. All my arguments, my demands, my unwillingness to fall in with your plans—I didn't understand what was making me push so hard to resist you. None of it made sense. Hell, for the past few years, I've tried to think up a legitimate excuse to move off the Silver Horn. Then when you gave me one, I fought against it, because I—well, I was afraid you were going to be like Bianca. And I wanted to test you, to see if you'd be willing to follow my wishes or start making demands like she did."

Still uncertain what he was trying to tell her, she shook her head. "Like Bianca? But, Evan, how could you think of me in that way? I'm not like her! I've never wanted money. For Pete's sake, I gave all of mine away!"

His hands came up to cradle the sides of her face. "I don't mean the money. Bianca shattered my trust, along with my self-confidence as a man and a detective. After she broke our engagement, I began to wonder whether any woman would ever love me just for me. Or if they simply loved the fact that I was a Calhoun, a member of one of the richest families in western Nevada. Then you came along, and you were so different from Bianca and the other women I'd dated. I could see that my money didn't impress you, but deep down I guess I still had doubts. I needed to know that I was the most important thing in your life. That you'd be willing to give up anything for me. I pushed you into a corner—unfairly so. I said hurtful things to you that I regret. Now I can only ask you to forgive me. To say you still love me."

Noelle's heart was suddenly brimming with such joy that she had to fight to keep from weeping. "I said plenty of awful things to you, too. But I'll try to make up for them by telling you how much I still love you. Very much."

"Oh, Elle, Elle, if I don't kiss you, I think I'm going to burst," he whispered, then fastened his lips over hers.

The passionate kiss went on and on as they tried to make up for all the heartache of the past few days.

When they finally broke for air, Evan said, "I still have your Christmas gift, but Vincent says I should exchange it for a solitaire—something more modest."

"Why would you want to do that?"

He nuzzled her cheek. "You said it didn't fit you."

"The ring is beautiful—now that I know it represents real love."

"Then you'll accept it? You'll marry me?"

Laughing softly, she wound her arms tightly around his neck. "Is it too late to say merry Christmas, darling?"

"Elle, my sweet, the gift of Christmas love is going to be with us all year round and for the rest of our lives."

Epilogue

Almost a year later, Noelle stood in front of the full-length mirror, adjusting the belt on her long suede skirt. The black color was slimming, but it still couldn't hide her rounded tummy.

"Evan, do you think I should change into something looser before we leave for your grandparents'? If you plan to surprise Tuck and Alice about the baby, then I can't walk in wearing this outfit. They'll take one look at my bulging belly and guess."

Crossing the little bedroom, Evan walked up behind his wife and slid his hands gently over her growing tummy. "Don't change. You look beautiful. And if they guess before I have a chance to tell them, then it won't matter. They'll be just as happy."

Turning to face her husband, she slipped her arms around his waist. "And what about you, my darling? Next month we'll have been married a year. Are you still happy?"

His soft laugh full of love and longing, he rested his forehead against hers. "If I was any happier, I couldn't stand myself. I'm making Vincent sick with all this talk about love and babies and ranching."

She laughed. "Ranching. It still sounds odd for you to say that word."

"Why? In my spare time away from the office, I'm

getting back into the groove of being a cowboy. And I've got to admit, Noelle, I'm beginning to like it. Especially when I have my beautiful wife working at my side."

She shot him an impish smile. "Beautiful? Evan, marriage has ruined your vision. Next thing I know, you'll be getting a new prescription and wondering what you ever saw in me."

Chuckling, he lifted her hand to his lips and kissed the callused area along the upper ridge of her palm. "I love every inch of you."

She sighed with contentment. "So much has happened since last Christmas. We had a beautiful wedding and reception on the Silver Horn. Sassy and Jett now have a daughter to go along with their little boy, J.J. Clancy and Olivia became parents to a baby boy, and the three of them have already moved into their dream house on Rock Mountain. And Lilly and Rafe have just welcomed another daughter into their family. Now I'm hearing that Bella's house is nearly finished. So she'll be moving into it soon. The family is shifting and growing and changing. But all for the good, don't you think?"

"Yes, all for the good. But you left out my move to this ranch," Evan pointed out. "That was the best change of all. You've taught me so much, my sweet wife. Like things don't have to be perfect to be good."

She cast a tender smile at him. "And you've taught me a lot about forgiving myself and others. I'm even thinking that I'll let my parents know about our baby. They deserve that much from me. And who knows? Maybe someday they'll come to realize the mistakes they made with their children."

"I'm glad," he said. "And I'm happy that my dad and

grandfather understand I'm truly content here on our own little ranch."

"Me, too," Noelle agreed. "Even though I think Bart is still getting used to not having you live on the Silver Horn anymore. But he seems to be taking it fairly well. You know, your grandfather called me yesterday and said he had a special gift for us this Christmas. I have a sneaky suspicion it's an Angus bull. What are we going to do? Turn it down?"

Shaking his head, Evan turned away from her and reached for his cowboy boots. As he sat on a footstool to jerk them on, he said, "No. We're going to take it. Sometimes accepting a gift graciously and gratefully means more than giving one. It will make him very happy, Elle. And it's not like we take advantage of his generosity. He's still trying to get you to take those hundred and fifty mama cows he offered after your cattle were stolen."

Reaching for the hairbrush on her dresser, she thoughtfully tugged it through her long hair. "Having the cattle stolen almost seems like a distant nightmare now. If you weren't such a good detective, you would've never caught the culprits who took them."

"Billy Stivers is the one to thank. Not only for giving me enough information to recover your cattle, but also for giving us a lead that eventually helped us solve the Watson homicide. Like Vince and I had thought all along, the crimes of the cattle rustling and the murder were connected. Watson was killed because he wanted more money for hauling the stolen cattle with his tractor-trailer rig. When his partner refused to pay up, Watson threatened to squeal to the authorities. Unfortunately, a syringe full of phenylbutazone shut him up before he could do that."

"Thank goodness the whole bunch is behind bars now," she said. "And from what you say, Billy Stivers is keeping his nose clean and out of trouble. I'm glad about that. Especially for Bernice's sake. She's such a good, gentle woman."

"I think Watson's death flipped on a light switch in Billy's head. He suddenly realized that if you run with an outlaw, you sometimes die like an outlaw."

"Speaking of outlaws, I've been doing plenty of thinking about my brother's accident. I—"

"Elle," Evan interrupted with surprise. "That's the first time I've heard you call your brother's death an accident. Does that mean—"

"It means that I've faced the truth of the matter. Andy wasn't a totally guiltless victim. He'd chosen to run with bad company and to put himself in a dangerous situation. And this past year, I've thought a lot about how you could be faced with a crazed gunman or knife-wielding criminal. I'd want you to protect yourself. Just like the policeman who killed Andy was trying to protect himself and any innocent bystanders."

Rising from the footstool, Evan curled an arm around her thickening waist. "Does that mean that you've forgiven the officer?"

Nodding, she looked into his eyes and smiled. "Forgiveness is freeing. Thank you, darling, for helping me understand that."

"I'm so proud of you. You're an incredible woman. My woman." Bending his head, he kissed her tenderly, then eased back far enough to give her a smile. "Are you ready to go? Granddad and Grandmother are expecting us for lunch. We'd better get a move on if we're going to make it by noon."

"Is Alice cooking chicken and dumplings?" Noelle

asked eagerly. "If she is, I want you to get me there as fast as the law allows."

Evan laughed. "So you haven't forgotten how good her dumplings are."

Turning, she tilted her face up to his. "I haven't forgotten anything about that day you took me to Virginia City to visit your grandparents. I not only fell deeper in love with you but also got a glimpse of what it was like to celebrate Christmas with a real family."

He pressed a light kiss to her lips. "And now the two of us are making our own real family. Years from now, our grandchildren will come to visit us during the holidays and introduce their dates, and you and I will think back to how it was when we were young and falling in love."

"Yes," she whispered with a dreamy smile. "We'll think back and remember that very special Christmas."

* * * * *

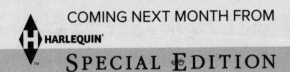

REQUEST YOUR FREE BOOKS!
2 FREE NOVELS PLUS 2 FREE GIFTS!

(H) HARLEQUIN®

SPECIAL EDITION
Life, Love & Family

HSE13R

SPECIAL EDITION

*Jensen Fortune Chesterfield is only in
Horseback Hollow, Texas, to see his new niece...not
get lassoed by a cowgirl! Amber Rogers isn't the kind
of woman Jensen ever imagined falling for. But, as
Amber's warm heart and outgoing ways melt his heart,
the handsome aristocrat begins to wonder if he might
find true love on the range after all...*

***

"What...was...that...kiss?" She stopped, her words coming out in raspy little gasps.

"...all about?" he finished for her.

She merely nodded.

"I don't know. It just seemed like an easier thing to do than to talk about it."

Maybe so, but being with Jensen was still pretty clandestine, what with meeting in the shadows, under the cloak of darkness.

The British Royal and the Cowgirl. They might be attracted to each other—and she might be good enough for him to entertain the idea of a few kisses in private or even a brief, heated affair. And maybe she ought to consider the same thing for herself, too.

But it would never last. Especially if the press—or the town gossips—got wind of it.

So she shook it all off—the secretive nature of it all, as well as the sparks and the chemistry, and opened the passenger door. "Good night, Jensen."

"What about dinner?" he asked. "I still owe you, remember?"

Yep, she remembered. Trouble was, she was afraid if she got in any deeper with him, there'd be a lot she'd have a hard time forgetting.

"We'll talk about it later," she said.

"Tomorrow?"

"Sure. Why not?"

"I may have to take my brother and sister to the airport, although I'm not sure when. I'll have to find out. Maybe we can set something up after I get home."

"Maybe so." She wasn't going to count on it, though. Especially when she had the feeling he wouldn't want to be seen out in public with her—where the newshounds or local gossips might spot them.

But as she headed for her car, she wondered if, when he set his mind on something, he might be as persistent as those pesky reporters he tried to avoid.

Well, Amber Rogers was no pushover. And if Jensen Fortune Chesterfield thought he'd met someone different from his usual fare, he didn't know the half of it. Because he'd more than met his match.

***

We hope you enjoyed this sneak peek at
A ROYAL FORTUNE by USA TODAY *bestselling*
author Judy Duarte, the first book in the brand-new
Harlequin® Special Edition continuity
THE FORTUNES OF TEXAS:
COWBOY COUNTRY!

On sale in January 2015, wherever
Harlequin Special Edition books and ebooks are sold.

JUST CAN'T GET ENOUGH
ROMANCE
Looking for more?

Harlequin has everything from contemporary, passionate and heartwarming to suspenseful and inspirational stories.

Whatever your mood, we have a romance just for you!

Connect with us to find your next great read, special offers and more.

Facebook.com/HarlequinBooks
Twitter.com/HarlequinBooks
HarlequinBlog.com
Harlequin.com/Newsletters

⬧ HARLEQUIN®

A *Romance* FOR EVERY MOOD™

www.Harlequin.com

SERIESHALOAD